"Our only chance is to get up this ladder to the street. Think you can make it?"

Framer shook his head. "Leave me here. I'm too weak."

The man's face was grayish. He needed medical attention soon, very soon. Bolan motioned for Grimaldi to go up first. Without another word he began scaling the iron rungs. Seconds later Grimaldi called down, "Clear up here so far."

Holstering the Beretta, the Executioner turned back to Framer. "Listen," Bolan said. "I'm going to climb up the ladder. You hold on to me with all you've got. Ready?"

Framer grunted a yes.

Bolan waited for the man to secure his grip, then began climbing. The extra weight made every movement difficult, but the soldier continued the rigorous assent. When they were halfway up, Bolan tried to count the number of rungs to the top. Perhaps fifteen more.

Fifteen, fourteen, thirteen—

The iron rung under his left hand popped loose from its cement socket.

Framer screamed.

Bolan managed to tighten his grip on the other rung he was still holding, avoiding the deadly plunge. Thirteen had always been his lucky number.

MACK BOLAN ®
The Executioner

THE EXECUTIONER

DON PENDLETON'S

UNCUT TERROR

A GOLD EAGLE BOOK FROM
WORLDWIDE®

TORONTO • NEW YORK • LONDON
AMSTERDAM • PARIS • SYDNEY • HAMBURG
STOCKHOLM • ATHENS • TOKYO • MILAN
MADRID • WARSAW • BUDAPEST • AUCKLAND

First edition October 2015

ISBN-13: 978-0-373-64443-8

Special thanks and acknowledgment to
Michael A. Black for his contribution to this work.

Uncut Terror

Recycling programs
for this product may
not exist in your area.

Wit must be foiled by wit; cut a diamond with a diamond.
—William Congreve

You can't reason with terrorists. The men and women who deal in violence and fear can only be stopped by action. That's where I come in.
—Mack Bolan

THE
MACK BOLAN
LEGEND

Nothing less than a war could have fashioned the destiny of the man called Mack Bolan. Bolan earned the Executioner title in the jungle hell of Vietnam.

But this soldier also wore another name—Sergeant Mercy. He was so tagged because of the compassion he showed to wounded comrades-in-arms and Vietnamese civilians.

Mack Bolan's second tour of duty ended prematurely when he was given emergency leave to return home and bury his family, victims of the Mob. Then he declared a one-man war against the Mafia.

He confronted the Families head-on from coast to coast, and soon a hope of victory began to appear. But Bolan had broken society's every rule. That same society started gunning for this elusive warrior—to no avail.

So Bolan was offered amnesty to work within the system against terrorism. This time, as an employee of Uncle Sam, Bolan became Colonel John Phoenix. With a command center at Stony Man Farm in Virginia, he and his new allies—Able Team and Phoenix Force—waged relentless war on a new adversary: the KGB.

But when his one true love, April Rose, died at the hands of the Soviet terror machine, Bolan severed all ties with Establishment authority.

Now, after a lengthy lone-wolf struggle and much soul-searching, the Executioner has agreed to enter an "arm's-length" alliance with his government once more, reserving the right to pursue personal missions in his Everlasting War.

Prologue

Krasnoyarsk Province, Siberia

VASSILI STIEGLITZ, DEPUTY MINISTER of economic affairs, watched the bleak countryside flash past the window of the state sedan that had been waiting for him at the airport. Snow-capped mountains loomed in the distance and, as they passed through the small village on the outskirts of the prison, Stieglitz noticed the furtive glances from those walking or pedaling along the road. This remote place was the land of peasants. Those who didn't eke out their pathetic existence in the factories or shops worked at the detention facility. The huge walls of the prison were not yet visible, but Stieglitz was in no hurry to get there. His assignment was explicit, and failure was not an option.

His satellite phone jangled, startling him. He had assumed he'd be unreachable this far from civilization. But he knew the power of the Kremlin was limitless. He answered the phone and immediately felt a quiver run down his spine when he heard the voice on the other end.

"Have you arrived yet?"

"No," Stieglitz said, hesitating to add more. The driver, although doubtlessly handpicked, was still a set of ears Stieglitz didn't need. "I am almost there."

"Good. I have arranged for a little incentive." The man

on the other end of the line chuckled. "It is best to tenderize the meat before preparation."

Another shiver went down Stieglitz's spine. He replied with a banal agreement.

"Very well, comrade Stieglitz. Call me when your task has been completed."

Stieglitz assured the man that he would but realized he was speaking to dead air. He replaced the phone in his pocket and looked out the window again. The landscape appeared even harsher than before. "Tenderize the meat before preparation."

Seven months ago, once Stieglitz had been tasked with his part of the master plan, he had moved swiftly, having Grodovich transferred from Ariyskhe to the more stringent encampment of Krasnoyarsk. Although Grodovich's crime, failure to report and pay the proper taxes on his business earnings, was considered a lesser, nonviolent offense, the transfer had hopefully served its purpose. Being in the midst of murderers, rapists, robbers and the like had surely softened up the highly successful, yet unscrupulous, businessman.

Grodovich was looking at ten more years in a place commonly referred to as "hell on earth." Stieglitz wondered what kind of horrors the man had witnessed in the past seven months and shuddered at the thought. How could Grodovich not jump at the chance to be released? And not just a release…a presidential pardon, as well.

All for a nominal fee and his participation in the plan.

The sedan went by an old woman limping along, her filthy shawl drawn tightly around her lumpy body. Although it was only October, autumn for much of the world, the wind in this godforsaken place was like the encroaching tentacles of winter. Stieglitz had been told that the temperatures dropped to minus eleven degrees Celsius within the walls of Detention Center 6. The numbing cold would be enough to make the slick businessman amenable, even without his ties to the *mafiya*. How could it not?

Yes, he thought. The plan will work.

They sped past two more peasants huddling against the chilly mountain wind and Stieglitz told the driver to turn up the heat, even though he was already sweating under his heavy overcoat.

Yes, he told himself again. The plan will work. It has to.

1

Detention Center 6
Krasnoyarsk, Siberia

ALEXANDER GRODOVICH SAT on his bunk and watched as the four men squirmed on the bed next to the door. The others huddled in a semicircle. Two of the burlier ones held the new prisoner facedown on the bed, the man's pants bunched around his ankles, his buttocks exposed. Oleg, the chief tattoo artist of Krasnoyarsk, flashed a gap-toothed grin at Grodovich as he dipped the makeshift needle into the cup of ink and bent over the prone man. Oleg pinched the soft, flabby skin between his forefinger and thumb and began the quick piercing that would imbue the ink onto the man's buttocks. The picture of a huge, open eye and partial nostril seemed to stare back at Grodovich.

He felt no pity for the restrained prisoner, who was being labeled as a provider of sexual gratification. After all, the man was a child molester.

The prisoner squealed as the pointed metal pricked his skin. Oleg laughed and gave the soft flesh a quick slap.

"Be still," he said. "Or we'll turn you into a eunuch, as well."

The others laughed, too. One of them turned toward

Grodovich with a knowing cackle, but the leering grin quickly faded as Mikhal stood up from his bunk.

Grodovich glanced at his hulking protector and smiled. Upon his unexpected transfer from Ariyskhe, Grodovich had immediately put his monetary resources to work, first bribing the guards to be kept in isolation, while scouring the prison for a suitable protector.

"You want Mikhal Markovich," the head guard whispered to him through the cell door. "He's serving a life sentence for murdering ten people, but he has a mother in Novosibirsk who comes to see him every month. She scrubs floors in the railway stations for a pittance and still brings us rubles each month so we'll give him extra rations." The guard grunted. "When you see him, you'll know why she is concerned. He is a giant."

And so he was. Huge in body but simple in the head, as the guard had explained. But this lack of guile, this simplicity, made him among the most feared inmates in Krasnoyarsk. He was oblivious to pain and completely without compassion or fear. And he was serving a life sentence. Bother him and you could be assured he would strike back without concern for punishment or retaliation. Mikhal had already killed three men inside the walls. These deaths were the result of the secret prisoner fights the guards held periodically. With a few payments to the guards and a series of monetary gifts to Mikhal's mother, that giant quickly assumed the role of Grodovich's protector. Fiercely loyal, he made sure that the only tattoos Grodovich received were the eight-pointed stars on his chest and knees that assured he would not be bothered inside the walls of Krasnoyarsk.

The new prisoner squealed again, begging for them to stop, which elicited more laughter from the group.

"Soon you'll be getting all the attention you can handle," one of them said.

A whistle sounded from the hall and an electric current shot through the dormitory room.

The guards were approaching.

Oleg quickly stepped back and shoved the cup of ink and the "needle" under the mattress of an adjacent bunk. The two men holding the child molester released him and motioned for him to pull up his pants.

The door burst open as the prisoner was buckling his trousers. All the men stood at attention as the three uniformed guards, armed with heavy black batons, entered the room and looked around. The lead guard's gaze settled on Grodovich.

"You," the guard said. "Come with us."

Mikhal turned his huge head toward the man, and the guard's face registered a bit of alarm.

"What is this about?" Grodovich asked.

"You have a visitor," the guard said. "An official one."

Grodovich considered this. He wasn't expecting anyone. His lawyer came once a month to attend to his needs, and deliver the bribes to his keepers, but he'd been here less than a week ago. Still, a visitor was always a welcome diversion. He stood and grabbed his cap from the post on his bed. Mikhal picked up his cap, as well.

"Not him," the guard said, pointing at the giant. "Just you."

Grodovich smiled and placed a hand on Mikhal's massive shoulder.

"Wherever I go," he said, "he goes."

The guards looked at each other. One of them glanced at the urine stain on the bed, then to the impassive faces of the line of prisoners.

"Not this time," the chief guard said. "Orders. Just you. The front office. Let's go. Now."

Grodovich felt the muscles of the giant's arm tensing. Still, a confrontation with the guards would put him in solitary confinement. Grodovich smiled and patted Mikhal's arm gently.

"It is all right, my friend," he said. "I will see you when I return."

Grodovich squared his hat on his head as they headed for the door. The three guards followed, ushering him down a long corridor flanked by dormitory rooms on the right and windows covered with heavy metal screening on the left. The light that managed to filter through the encrusted filth on the panes dappled the mustard yellow walls. A myriad of dust motes floated in the speckles of sunshine. They came to the end of the corridor and moved down the stairwell toward the third floor. At the second landing, the ranking guard told everyone to halt. He turned and looked at Grodovich, who noticed that the man's face was now damp.

The hairs on the back of Grodovich's neck rose. He thought about calling out for Mikhal but doubted the giant could get there fast enough.

"What is going on?" Grodovich asked. "Didn't you receive your monthly payment?"

The ranking guard said nothing. He pursed his lips and motioned toward the stairway.

"Go wait for us down there," the guard said, pointing to the dimly lighted first-floor landing. "We have to attend to something on the second floor."

"Attend to what?"

"An emergency," the guard said. "Now go." He and the others immediately opened the door and ran into the hallway.

Grodovich stood there, listening to the fading sound of their boots on the tiled floor.

Someone was waiting for him down there. Had he been marked for death, and if so, by whom? He began to creep back up the stairway, careful not to make too much noise. From the floor above he heard a low whisper and then a laugh. A swarthy face appeared around the corner, a gap-toothed smile stretched across it. Grodovich recognized the man as a fellow inmate, a Chechen.

The man held up his left hand and waggled his fingers, making a come-hither gesture. He stepped fully into the landing and Grodovich saw the man's right hand held a long, metallic blade, probably fashioned from one of the soup cups.

Grodovich turned and ran down the stairs toward the second-floor landing. Should he try to summon the guards?

No, they had set him up. They would do nothing to help him now.

He rounded the corner and continued his descent toward the first floor. Suddenly three more Chechens appeared, blocking his path. Each one held a crude blade. Each one smiled.

Grodovich froze. He stooped and reached for his own shank, a thin strip of metal that he'd managed to liberate from the sole of a worn shoe, but he was inept at using it. Still, he would not go down without a fight. He backed into the corner of the landing as the four men approached from both above and below.

"What is this?" Grodovich asked. "I have done nothing to offend you."

"We have our orders," one of the Chechens said as he continued creeping up from the first floor. "It is nothing of a personal—"

A sudden gurgling interrupted everything. Grodovich glanced up in time to see a huge hand encircling the throat of the Chechen who'd been coming down from the third floor. He attempted to stab the big hand, but another large hand closed over that one. The man struggled like a puppet as his feet dangled and swung in open air, then all movement stopped. Mikhal's enormous form became visible behind him. The giant picked up the strangled marionette and held him at chest level while he strode down the stairs. When Mikhal reached the second-floor landing he flung the dead man toward the other three.

One of them was knocked off his feet, another staggered back. The third one, the closest, made a lunging stab with his blade.

Mikhal stepped back with the agility of an acrobat and seized the Chechen's wrist. Seconds later the man howled in pain. Mikhal forced the Chechen's knife back into his throat and let him drop to the floor, lumbering toward the two others. They both scrambled down the stairway with Mikhal in pursuit. Grodovich glanced around, then called to him.

"Wait," he said. "Don't chase them. It could be a trap."

The giant halted, his face flushed with exertion, his breathing hard.

"I felt I should follow you," Mikhal said. He seldom spoke, and when he did his voice sounded almost childlike. "I looked down the hall and saw that Chechen bastard sneaking around."

"I'm glad you did, my friend. Once again, you have saved my life." Grodovich heard the thudding of boots coming from the second-floor hallway. He motioned upward and told Mikhal to run. "If the guards see you here, they will use it as an excuse to place you in the solitary ward. Go."

The giant hesitated for a split second, then strode up

the stairs, taking them three at a time. Grodovich tossed his own blade and pressed himself into the corner of the landing. The door burst open and three different guards emerged.

"What is going on here?" the ranking guard yelled, his eyes widening as he surveyed the scene.

"A disagreement between two inmates," Grodovich said. "They fought and killed each other. It was terrible to behold."

The guard's mouth worked, but no words came out. He licked his lips, pulled out his radio and spoke into it with clear precise tones, ordering more men to come to his position. He scrutinized Grodovich, who held up his hands to show there were no traces of blood.

"Some of your compatriots were taking me to see an official visitor when they had to leave," he said with a smile. "I hope their emergency has run its course without incident."

Judo Training Center
Arlington, Virginia

MACK BOLAN, the Executioner, sat on the edge of the mat and watched as the judo master demonstrated the last few techniques, throwing his much younger partner around with ease. The *gi* felt heavy on Bolan's shoulders. He preferred to train in his regular clothes, wearing his standard gear, but the owner of the dojo had insisted that all attendees had to wear the traditional judo garb. It was a small price to pay for being able to see a master such as Kioshi Watinabi at work.

Jack Grimaldi, who was seated next to Bolan, leaned over and whispered, "Ah, it looks like the one guy's faking it."

Bolan shook his head and brought his index finger to his lips.

"Whatever," Grimaldi said sotto voce. He leaned back and sighed.

Bolan watched as the master executed the final move, *Hiza Guruma*, the wheeling knee throw. As the opponent stepped forward, the master stepped back and smacked the sole of his left foot against the other man's knee. Twisting the opponent's upper body in a circular motion, the master sent the other man over with a quick flip.

Grimaldi snorted. "Like I said, all fake."

Bolan shot him another quieting look, but it was obvious the judo master, an Asian man in his fifties, had already cast a glance their way. His eyebrows lifted slightly as he stared at Grimaldi. Then the master and his opponent bowed to each other, turned and bowed again to the audience.

Grimaldi stretched and yawned. "Ready to blow this pop stand?"

Before Bolan could answer the master held up his hands and waggled his fingers for the rest of the class to move forward, saying something in Japanese.

"The master wishes you to pair up for individual instruction," the young assistant said.

The group of spectators got up and shuffled to the center mat. Bolan and Grimaldi paired off and gripped the thick lapels of each other's *gis*. The master called out commands for each technique. The first was *O Goshi*, the major hip throw. The second was *Harai Goshi*, sweeping hip throw.

"You want to go first?" Bolan asked.

Grimaldi shook his head. "Nah. I want to prove to you that this stuff doesn't work. It's just like professional wrestling."

"Okay," Bolan said and pivoted, pulling Grimaldi off balance and stepping inside his guard. Bolan slipped his right hip against Grimaldi's abdomen as he stepped back with his left foot and twisted, throwing Grimaldi over with a quick flip.

Grimaldi slammed onto the mat, managing to break his fall with a slapping motion of his left arm.

"You all right?" Bolan asked.

Grimaldi grunted. "I know how to fall."

Master Watinabi strode over to them, speaking in Japanese and motioning for Grimaldi to get to his feet. As he did the master continued to give instructions to Bolan along with numerous gestures. The young assistant began translating.

"Master Watinabi says your technique is very good," he said to Bolan. "But he suggests bending lower if the opponent resists." He turned to Grimaldi and said, "Stiffen your arms."

Grimaldi grinned and locked his arms, which were much longer than Watinabi's. The two men stepped back and forth and suddenly Watinabi thrust his right foot into Grimaldi's stomach and fell backward. Grimaldi flipped over and landed on his back with a thud. As he got up, Watinabi grabbed him once more, slipped into a modified hip throw and swept Grimaldi's legs out from under him, flipping him over on his back again. Grimaldi got up a bit slower this time and Watinabi grabbed him once more and thrust his hip into Grimaldi's stomach.

The master paused and the assistant said, "Grab his belt and attempt to lift him backward."

Grimaldi smiled and reared back, lifting the smaller man completely off the mat, but Watinabi lifted both of his legs to his chest then thrust them downward, at the same time grasping Grimaldi around the neck. As soon as Watinabi's feet struck the mat Grimaldi was launched over the master's right hip, his body flying pell-mell before slamming once again onto the mat.

He lay there trying to get his breath.

"That is a useful technique against a taller opponent," the assistant said.

Watinabi grinned at Grimaldi as Bolan reached to help him up.

"Good thing you know how to fall," Bolan said.

Before Grimaldi could respond with one of his standard wisecracks, a cell phone rang.

The Executioner glanced to the edge of the mat where his and Grimaldi's clothes and shoes had been stacked.

"Oh," Grimaldi said. "Saved by the bell. Is it yours or mine?"

"It must be yours. I turned mine off."

Grimaldi grinned as he lay back. "In that case I'm really saved by the bell."

"Don't be too sure," Bolan said. "It's probably Hal."

Detention Center 6
Krasnoyarsk, Siberia

THE GUARDS MARCHED on either side of Grodovich. They were near the front offices of the prison, this much Grodovich knew from his orientation seven months ago. This was only the second time he'd been so close to the entrance. What was going on?

Another transfer?

Perhaps they were sending him back to the less severe prison at Ariyskhe. After all, his crimes did not involve violence, only paper: conspiracy to avoid paying appropriate governmental fees and taxes and unethical business dealings. At least the crimes they knew about. There was no way he should have been transferred to Krasnoyarsk. He had never received an explanation as to why they'd placed him into this hellhole. But at Detention Center 6, one did not ask.

The lead guard stopped at a solid-looking door and lightly knocked three times.

Such deference indicated a person of no small importance was on the other side.

This piqued Grodovich's curiosity.

A voice from inside the room told them to enter. The lead guard motioned for Grodovich to place his hands on the wall and assume the search position. Grodovich complied and felt the hands of the other two guards squeeze every part of his body with practiced efficiency. He was used to the indignities of life behind the walls and was glad he'd dropped his blade in the stairwell, for they surely would have found it.

The aborted attack by the Chechens still floated before him. He'd done nothing to provoke them. Why had they accosted him, and why had the guards, to whom he paid protection each month, led him into such a clumsy trap? The answer was obvious. Someone had paid them more. But who, and more important, why?

The Chechen had muttered something right before Mikhal had terminated him: "We have our orders. It is nothing of a personal—"

What had he meant? And why had he said it?

A strange prelude for this meeting.

The lead guard opened the door and pointed for Grodovich to go in. He squared his black cap on his head and tugged his now misaligned clothing into a semblance of order. As he went inside the room he saw a thin man with a completely bald head and a pair of gold-rimmed glasses. The man wore a dark blue suit and his black shoes had a shine on them. He stood there watching and assessing as Grodovich entered and stood at attention. For the better part of thirty seconds, the bald man did not speak, then he took in a copious breath and motioned for Grodovich to sit in a nearby chair.

"I am Vassili Stieglitz from the interior ministry of economics," the man said. "And you are Alexander Grodovich."

Grodovich resisted the urge to comment. With the virtually endless sentence before him he had little to lose, but he had been incarcerated long enough to know that there was no sense throwing rocks at the gatekeepers. Besides, this meeting had some significance to bring an interior minister all the way from the Kremlin. Whatever this man wanted was worth finding out. There would be plenty of time for reflection on missed opportunities for sarcasm later, when he was back in the cell block.

Stieglitz inhaled again. "How do you like the facilities here in Krasnoyarsk?"

This was too much. The absurdity of the question made him laugh. "I have stayed in better."

Stieglitz raised his right eyebrow. "I'm certain that you have." He held Grodovich's stare for several seconds and then said, "And you still have a substantial sentence yet to serve."

Grodovich said nothing.

The bald man maintained his stare. "And what would you say if I offered you a way out?"

A shiver shot up Grodovich's spine. Was this some sort of trick? Was this man toying with him? What did he want? It had to be money. His Swiss accounts.

Grodovich had been expecting such a financial deal when he was first arrested, although the opportunity to negotiate never materialized. His lawyers told him that such a deal could be made, but the conditions were absurd: total capitulation. They offered him a penniless freedom, with no guarantees on their part. He would either end up in prison or living as a beggar on the streets.

Thus, he'd held out, refusing to give up the numbers of his Swiss accounts. It was his only bargaining chip, because these bastards could not be trusted. The monthly bribes to the prison guards were still arriving on time, despite his transfer to Detention Center 6, and, most important, Mikhal's sainted mother received her monthly allotment in Novosibirsk.

The first few days of Grodovich's arrival had been hell, but still, he had survived. This was no doubt round two. The transfer to the more brutal surroundings had been a prelude to soften him up. So this was a negotiation, and he must show strength. He could not let this bald government rodent know his desperation.

Grodovich took his time before answering. "I would indeed be interested, but it would depend."

Stieglitz's brow furrowed. "Depend upon what?"

Grodovich managed to smile. He'd regained a modicum of self-respect, if not some purchase on the slope of the negotiation.

"Upon the nature of your request," Grodovich said. "You obviously wish something from me, the cost of which must be evaluated before any decision can be made."

"Are you mad?" the bald man asked. "I'm offering you a way out of this hellhole and you have the audacity to attempt to set the conditions?"

Grodovich smiled again. He was indeed gaining purchase. "Everything," he said, "even life in here, has conditions."

Stieglitz snorted. "I do not have time for games."

"All I have is time," Grodovich answered. He kept his

expression bland. It was like a game of chess, waiting for your opponent to make the move that allowed first blood.

Stieglitz clasped his hands behind his back and strode to a dirt-streaked window covered with an iron grate. He stared through the filthy glass for several seconds. "All right," he said finally, turning back to face him. "I can appreciate that you have been toughened by your incarceration. But let me assure you I did not come all the way from Moscow to play games. I am, quite simply, offering you your freedom. A presidential pardon for your crimes. Immediate, total and absolute freedom."

Grodovich could hardly believe it. But he waited for the other shoe to drop, and he was betting it had a steel sole. He tried his best to conceal his excitement, wondering what the cost would be. Still, he knew it really did not matter. At this point he would sell his mother's soul if it got him out of here a day quicker. But to show weakness in a negotiation was tantamount to capitulation. He composed himself and said, "What exactly must I do in exchange for this pardon?"

The corner of Stieglitz's mouth tweaked, like a flicker from a hungry, feral cat, and he smiled. "We would like you to renew your old contacts on the international front as you go back into the diamond business." He paused. "And with the Robie Cats."

Stony Man Farm
Virginia

As BOLAN AND GRIMALDI entered the War Room, Bolan noticed two steaming cups of coffee on the front edge of the table. Hal Brognola leaned back in his chair as he sipped from his own mug with a sour expression stretched across his face.

"I told you we should've stopped by Starbucks," Grimaldi said, grinning. "I take it Aaron whipped up his customary brew?"

Brognola swallowed and gave his head a quick shake. Then he looked toward the door, checking to see whether Aaron "The Bear" Kurtzman, Stony Man's computer expert, was close by. "Worse. You could use this batch to clean rust off a spark plug." He indicated the two empty chairs in front of the desk.

Bolan sat down, leaving the cup where it was. He knew better than to sample it.

Grimaldi took a tentative sip from his and howled. "Damn, you could pour this into an old deuce-and-a-half if you ran out of gas."

"What's up?" Bolan asked. "We left a very interesting judo seminar to be here."

"Judo seminar?" Brognola said. "Don't you guys get enough practice beating people up?"

"You know the motto of our superhero here," Grimaldi said, motioning toward Bolan. "It's never too late to inflict some pain."

"Especially if you provoke the instructor," Bolan added.

Brognola laughed. "I can't wait to hear about that one." He set the mug down and cleared his throat. "But in the meantime, I have a favor to ask."

Bolan nodded. He was accustomed to such sudden requests. Usually they came to Brognola indirectly from the White House. Special details that were too hot to go through normal channels. From the look on Brognola's face, Bolan knew this one had the ring of immediacy and urgency. He waited for Grimaldi's customary wisecrack.

"A favor?" Grimaldi said. "Who'd a *thunk* it?"

Brognola leaned forward, placing his forearms on the

tabletop. "As I'm sure you're aware, things have been tense between us and Russia lately."

"Don't tell me our side finally realized the old reset button isn't working?" Grimaldi said.

"The current round of sanctions is causing a bit of havoc on their economy," Brognola said. "Just how much remains to be seen."

"You want us to fly to Moscow and check things out?" Grimaldi asked. "If so, I'd prefer to go now, before the winter sets in. That place is damn miserable then."

"A trip to Moscow is in the cards," Brognola said. He paused, picked up a remote and pressed a few buttons. A large screen began lowering from a metal roll on the opposite wall as the lights in the room became subdued. An overhead projector hummed to life and a bright, square patch was illuminated on the screen. Brognola pressed another button and a man's face appeared. He was dark haired, had with heavy acne scarring and was wearing dark sunglasses. "Look familiar?"

"Larry Burns," Bolan said. "The Kremlin's second favorite American defector."

"Don't tell me you want us to drag that little creep back here by the scruff of his neck," Grimaldi said. "It'd be my pleasure, but the Russians wouldn't let us get within spitting distance of him."

"Let's just say that Mr. Burns is ready to come home," Brognola said. "He's been secretly meeting with our Agency personnel for the past two weeks."

"Why don't they just take him to the Embassy?" Bolan asked. "I'm sure the Russians have already gotten everything they need out of him."

"Ordinarily, that would be the plan." Brognola clicked the remote again and another male appeared on the screen.

This one was a rather portly man with glasses and blond hair. "Except for this guy. Arkadi Kropotkan."

"Doesn't look like your typical FSB thug guard," Grimaldi said.

"He's not," Brognola replied. "He works for the Kremlin in the Bureau of Economic Affairs. Typical mild-mannered bureaucrat, except for one little thing." Brognola paused. "He happens to be quite close to our star defector."

Bolan studied the image on the screen, committing it to memory.

"How close is close?" Grimaldi asked.

Brognola sipped his coffee again before answering. "Let's just say they know each other in the Biblical sense of the word."

Grimaldi snorted. "I'll bet that's going over like a lead balloon, considering how the Kremlin feels about homosexuals."

"Apparently, the Kremlin doesn't know about it yet." Brognola set his mug down as he leaned forward. "And that's exactly why Mr. Burns wants to come home."

"And he wants to bring Kropotkin with him," Bolan said.

Brognola nodded. "Exactly. That's one of his conditions."

"Conditions?" Grimaldi said. "Since when does some turncoat defector get to set conditions with us?"

Brognola shrugged. "I agree with you, but he's also let on that Kropotkin is a wealth of information and has something significant to trade."

"So the Agency needs us to help get them both out?" Bolan asked.

Brognola nodded. "We've arranged for both of you to be sent there as sports reporters to cover the International Martial Arts Tournament being hosted this week. As you know, the Russian president is a big judo fan, and he'll be making some appearances at the tournament."

"So I've heard," Bolan said.

"Aaron's setting everything up," Brognola continued. "If you guys can assist the Agency in the operation, the President and I will be very appreciative."

"When do we leave?" Bolan asked.

Krasnoyarsk Province, Siberia

GRODOVICH WATCHED WITH amusement as Mikhal's huge hands fumbled with the seat belt. The center armrest in the airplane had been retracted to accommodate his immense frame, but now he struggled trying to figure out how to insert the metal flange into the buckle. Grodovich realized that Mikhal had most likely never been on an airplane before. He had never driven a car, either, and the only vehicles he'd ridden in were the bus that had taken him to prison and the van that had transported them from Detention Center 6 to this airport, where Stieglitz's jet had been waiting.

A private jet, Grodovich thought. Interesting and elucidating. Some heavy hitters were involved in this scheme.

The pretty flight attendant smiled as she gently took the two parts from Mikhal and connected them, then showed him how to pull on the excess to tighten it. The giant recoiled at her touch, and this further amused Grodovich. He wondered if his huge friend had ever experienced the pleasure of a woman's body. From the big man's uneasiness, he doubted it. After all, Mikhal had been imprisoned since his mid-teens, and he was now around thirty. The landscape of tattoos covering his massive body told of his journey through the penal system.

Grodovich recalled how long it had been for him, as

well. How long he'd been incarcerated, and how long it had been since he'd had a woman. Soon that would be rectified…for both of them.

Stieglitz had initially balked at the idea of releasing Mikhal, but Grodovich countered that the condition was non-negotiable. It had been a risk, that was certain, but one worth taking. Grodovich had sensed that it was one of the rare instances when he might have the upper hand. Stieglitz had not journeyed all the way from Moscow to not bring back the prize his superiors wanted. Grodovich also knew his ability to dictate terms would fade quickly once he was out and under a new form of control. Thus, having someone at his side, someone he could trust, would be Grodovich's only real assurance. He knew that if the time came when his new masters decided they no longer needed him, the payoff would probably be a bullet to the head. With Mikhal, he stood a fair chance of survival beyond the completion of this scheme. In the meantime, he had only to enjoy his newly found freedom.

Relax, he thought as he watched big Mikhal squirming in the seat as the flight attendant's hand rested on his shoulder.

She wore jeweled earrings that glistened under the cabin's lights, and this brought Grodovich back to the original question he had posed: What exactly must he do in exchange for this pardon?

"We would like you to renew your old contacts on the international front as you go back into the diamond business…and with the Robie Cats," Stieglitz had said.

What exactly did that mean? The Robies had sprung up the last two years, mostly while he'd been imprisoned. They were essentially an instrument of his former partner, who'd formed the group and sponsored them. They had become as adept at stealing jewels as their fictional inspiration, John Robie, from that old movie.

Grodovich turned and peered through the oval window at Stieglitz, who had yet to board the plane. He was still standing on the tarmac by the stairway talking on his mobile phone, and from the man's body language he was obviously speaking to whoever was in charge of this farce. Initially, Grodovich had wondered if the Chechen stooges had been sent by Stieglitz to add an incentive to accept the offer. The transfer from Ariyskhe could have been designed to produce the same effect. Those in control had obviously arranged the chess pieces on the board in a particular manner and planned their moves well in advance. He wondered which one he was. The intricate manipulations indicated he was far more than a pawn... A knight, perhaps? Or maybe even a bishop?

The flight attendant tugged Mikhal's seat belt snuggly across his hips and the giant responded with a foul-smelling burst of flatulence.

The woman's head jerked back and she smiled before scurrying off.

Grodovich laughed. As rancid as it was, he and Mikhal were both breathing free air. And he intended to keep breathing it, despite any temporary effluviums that might drift his way.

"I am sorry, Alexander," Mikhal said. "I could not help myself. Have I offended her?"

Grodovich placed his hand on the giant's meaty thigh and gave it an affectionate squeeze.

"Do not concern yourself," he said. "Soon we will be in Moscow and partaking in pleasures you have only dreamed about."

The huge face twisted into a smile. "I have been thinking about that." The giant licked his lips, and then his massive visage took on a serious expression. "I will never forget that I owe you for my freedom."

Grodovich squeezed the enormous leg again. It was like the trunk of an oak tree. He nodded in reassurance but said nothing.

A knight or a bishop, he thought. It matters not when I have my own loyal rook.

STIEGLITZ STOOD SHIVERING in the cold wind that blew along the length of the airfield as the voice on the other end of the connection spoke with slow deliberation.

"I assume that everything went as I instructed?"

"Yes, sir," Stieglitz said. He felt the pressure growing in his bowels. Just hearing the other voice did that to him. He knew he could be exterminated in the blink of an eye.

Should he tell his superior about Grodovich's condition, the release of the giant, or keep that to himself? He'd been under orders to enlist Grodovich's cooperation using any means necessary. But Stieglitz had not been prepared for the intrusion of the giant, nor had he anticipated the audacity of Grodovich.

"Are you there?" The voice was petulant.

Not wanting to incur any wrath, Stieglitz answered quickly. "Yes, yes, of course. I'm on the airfield and they're fueling the plane now."

After a few seconds of silence, the voice came back on the line. "How much have you told him?"

"Only that we have a special assignment for him involving diamonds."

"We? You told him of my involvement?"

"No, no, of course not." Stieglitz felt himself almost lose control and void himself. "I was merely using a figure of speech."

More silence.

"As far as he knows," Stieglitz continued, "I am the one in charge."

Stieglitz heard nothing. Had the connection been lost? Was his death being ordered? Then, "Very well. Tell him what I instructed you to tell him. I have arranged for Rovalev to meet your plane in Moscow."

Rovalev, the Black Wolf. He would most assuredly report the matter of the giant being released. Stieglitz had to do the same, lest it seem as if he were concealing something.

"There is one more matter," he said nervously.

"What?"

Stieglitz tried to swallow, his mouth suddenly very dry, his hands so wet he was worried the special phone would slip from his grasp. "Grodovich wanted another convict, his...his companion, to be released, as well. I...uh...did that to appease him."

He listened to dead air for several seconds until the voice spoke again.

"His companion?" A harsh laugh. "Perhaps it will make him more amenable. After all, a happy man is an efficient one. And if there are any problems, Rovalev can handle it."

"Yes, of course, sir," Stieglitz said, thinking of the subsequent reaction to the giant.

"Is there anything else?"

"No, nothing, sir," he said. "Everything is as you instructed. Everything is under control."

"It had better be." The voice sounded cool, efficient, merciless. "Call me when you land."

Stieglitz felt relief flood through him as he terminated the call. He glanced up the metal stairway leading to the open door of the plane and debated whether or not he could ascend it without voiding. He decided against it and began a shuffling walk back toward the gate. They would not take off without him.

As he continued toward the structure he caught a glimpse of a face watching him through the window of the plane.

Grodovich.

It was a mistake to show weakness in front of this unctuous gangster, and Stieglitz hoped his truncated steps would not betray his anxiety.

Perhaps he will assume I am a nervous flier, he thought.

2

Somewhere over Germany
33,000 Feet

BOLAN HAD MANAGED to sleep in fits and starts over the course of the flight from New York. A few times he feigned sleep to escape Grimaldi's comments about how he could have flown the plane more efficiently. Finally, once his partner had drifted into a deep slumber, accompanied by some heavy snoring, Bolan straightened his seat and turned on the dome light. The flight attendant, a cheerful brunette, came by and asked if she could get him anything. Her English was tinctured with a heavy German accent. Bolan ordered a coffee.

He and Grimaldi were scheduled to arrive in Moscow at 0345, Tuesday morning. They'd left New York on Monday, so they'd lost a day to transit. Once they landed the plan was to get through customs as quickly as possible. Bolan fully expected their equipment would be scrutinized by the officials.

Lawrence Burns, a former employee of the NSA, had defected to Russia from his post in Manheim, Germany, citing a "crisis of conscience" with US policies toward the rest of the world. Burns had worked in the intelligence di-

vision and had been privy to a lot of top-secret messages
and computer files. The extent of his betrayal was still
being assessed, even after almost a year and a half. This
probably explained why the Agency had requested "outside" help bringing the traitor back. Many agents, sources
and assets had not doubt been compromised by the defection. Thus, the president's overture to Hal Brognola for
some special assistance now that Burns wished to return
to the country he'd once betrayed.

Bolan had little use for traitors, but he understood the
government's eagerness to get Burns back in the United
States. Without knowing exactly how much he'd told the
Russians in exchange for his asylum, the real damage
could only be speculated. A full accounting was indeed
in order. And the instructions to get both Burns and his
lover, Kropotkan, safely out of Russia meant that the G
planned on using the latter's immigration status as an in-
terrogation tool.

Cold, but effective.

The flight attendant brought him a cup full of steaming liquid. He smiled as he accepted it and thanked her.

"How much longer before we land, miss?" he asked,
lowering his tray table.

"It should be only another two hours, sir," she said.

"Two hours," Grimaldi said, rousing from his slumber.
"Heck, if I was flying this crate we'd be touching down
by now."

The flight attendant looked startled by his snarl.

"Yeah," Bolan said, sampling the coffee. "But we'd
probably be landing in Kiev instead."

Grimaldi snorted and readjusted his pillow. "The jokers
flying this thing shoulda stuck to piper cups. They must've
hit every bit of air turbulence over the damn Atlantic."

"Can I get you anything, sir?" the flight attendant asked. "Something to settle your stomach, perhaps?"

"Hey, babe," Grimaldi said, giving her the eye. "I left my stomach back over Hamburg, but I wouldn't mind taking you out for a drink when we land."

The flight attendant's cheeks reddened as she flashed a nervous smile and walked away.

"Aww, whatever," Grimaldi said, fluffing his pillow again. He resumed his recumbent position.

Good old Jack, Bolan thought as he drank more of the bitter coffee. Able to fly anything with wings or rotors and completely adept at being internationally disconcerting.

Moscow, Russia

THE MAN LOOKED lean but extremely powerful as he stood in the center of the large apartment. The building had once housed a factory but was converted to residential dwellings after the fall of the Soviet Union, when people began moving back into this section of the city. This particular dwelling could easily house two or three families. It was certainly much larger and more sumptuous than his own home. But then again, Stieglitz had no need of the extensive gymnasium equipment this one held.

He stood patiently as Boris Rovalev, also known in certain secret government corners as the Black Wolf, continued his assault of punches and kicks against a large, suspended canvas bag. The bag was the type boxers used but much longer. Its tail end hung only a few inches above the floor. Rovalev was shirtless and his body glistened with sweat. The hair on his back and shoulders made his nickname seem more appropriate, as did his lupine facial features—long nose, brownish-yellow eyes, swept-back dark hair and a thick but well-trimmed beard.

The bag continued to dance and jerk with each series of blows.

Stieglitz was in awe of the man's speed and power and silently wondered how he would fare if pitted against Mikhal. But whereas the giant's body was literally covered with tattoos the Black Wolf's skin was devoid of any such illustrations, a result of his having been selected for intelligence work by the FSB fifteen years ago. Rovalev had barely been out of high school when he was one of the finalists for the Russian Olympic boxing team. A sharp-eyed government agent realized the young man's talents could be put to better use after Rovalev methodically beat an older, more experienced opponent to the canvas after the man had floored him with a supposedly unintentional foul.

The Black Wolf delivered a series of punches to the heavy bag, stepped back and executed a spinning kick. As his foot smacked against the canvas the bag jerked from the power behind the blow.

Rovalev might just be able to beat the giant, Stieglitz thought, although it had undoubtedly been Mikhal who had decimated the three Chechens at Krasnoyarsk.

Stieglitz looked at his watch. Rovalev had insisted on completing his workout before discussing his assignment. Had his lack of deference been a deliberate sign of disrespect? Stieglitz wondered as he watched the Black Wolf deliver several more blows to the bag before stopping to strip off his gloves.

Finally, thought Stieglitz, but Rovalev was not yet ready to begin. Instead he ran past Stieglitz toward a pair of thick ropes that were suspended from the high ceiling next to a winding staircase. The Black Wolf grabbed the rope and went hand-over-hand up to the top, his legs held at a ninety-degree angle from his body. When he got to the top he paused and then did a quick descent. Again, Stieglitz glanced at his watch, more obviously this time. Didn't this low-level government FSB agent know to whom Stieglitz reported?

He cleared his throat as Rovalev dropped to the floor, his feet bare and covered with thick calluses. They looked like they could split a brick wall with ease.

"We have much to discuss," Stieglitz said. "And I am a bit pressed for time."

Rovalev stared back at him, silent and motionless.

Stieglitz suddenly felt an unsettling twinge in his gut and wished he'd brought his security detail with him, but that was impossible. His orders were clear: the secrecy of the plan was imperative. It was indeed like looking into the eyes of a feral wolf.

Finally, Rovalev broke their locked gaze as he turned and reached for a nearby towel. He wiped his face and upper torso.

"So what are your instructions?" Rovalev asked.

Stieglitz let out a slow breath and frowned.

The other man tossed the moist towel to the floor and it landed on top of Stieglitz's shoes.

"Do you know who I am?" he asked. "To whom I report? I could have you severely punished for your disrespect."

Rovalev smiled, his white teeth glinting in his swarthy face.

"And who would you send to do that?" he asked.

Stieglitz maintained his stare for several seconds before answering. If he didn't need this insolent bastard for the completion of the plan... It was clear he needed to pull out the big gun. He removed his mobile phone and punched in the special number.

The Black Wolf stared at him with a smile on his face.

The phone rang three times before the voice answered, "Yes?"

"I am sorry to disturb you, sir," Stieglitz said. His voice cracked as he spoke, and he tried to muster enough spittle to swallow. "I am having a bit of difficulty with Rovalev."

"Oh? What type of problem?"

Stieglitz glanced back at the yellowish-brown eyes staring at him with amusement.

"He does not seem to grasp the importance of this assignment," Stieglitz said.

"Give the phone to him."

Stieglitz handed the phone to Rovalev. "He wishes to speak to you."

The Black Wolf smirked as he accepted it and put it to his ear. "And who is this?"

Seconds later his jaw sagged slightly and his face paled. "Yes, sir." He seemed to become more erect, almost as if he were standing at attention. "Yes, sir, I understand completely… I am sorry for any misunderstanding, sir… I assure you, it will not happen again… Yes, sir, I shall do that… Thank you, sir. I look forward to serving with the utmost enthusiasm." He nodded, as if this would be visible through the mobile phone connection, mumbled another apology and assurance, then blinked as he handed the phone back to Stieglitz.

Stieglitz placed it next to his ear.

"It has been taken care of," the voice said. "Is there anything else?"

"No," Stieglitz said. "Thank you, sir."

The connection was terminated. Stieglitz replaced the mobile in its case and looked at the Black Wolf, raised an eyebrow, but said nothing. He waited for the other man to speak. When he did, it was the apology Stieglitz was expecting.

Stieglitz nodded slightly, letting the gravity of the phone call weigh on the other man's shoulders. Rovalev had been humbled, castigated, but perhaps he also surmised that he was to be an integral part of things. That would explain his initial audacity, so Stieglitz decided to come at him from a different direction, while still capitalizing on the advantage the phone call had wrought.

Perhaps it is time to appeal to this mercenary's venality, he thought, now that the metaphorical wave of Kremlin authority has washed over him. Stieglitz allowed a slow smile to lift the corners of his mouth.

"I must admit," he said, "you are everything I was informed you would be. I have reviewed your previous successes, especially in Chechnya and the Ukraine. I do hope, however, that your penchant for insolence does not override your ability to follow orders. As you now know, this is a matter of great importance to—" Here he paused again and allowed the Black Wolf's imagination to complete the sentence. "Also know that you will be compensated extremely well once the plan has been completed."

Now it was Rovalev's turn to look pensive. His amber-colored eyes darted down, then back to Stieglitz.

"What is it you wish me to do?" the Black Wolf asked.

Stieglitz smiled. He had him now. Asserting dominance over a professional killer was always a bit tricky until you found the proper method with which to demonstrate it.

"Assemble your usual team of associates," Stieglitz said. "You are to both guard and monitor a man. Two men, actually, but only one of them is significant to the plan."

"And these two men," Rovalev asked. "Who are they and what do they do?"

"That will all be explained shortly," Stieglitz said. "For now, you need only know that one of them is in the diamond business."

Rovalev nodded. "How soon do you need us?"

"Soon," Stieglitz said. "Very soon. There is another slight matter to which you must attend to shortly. A loose end that must be tied up."

The Black Wolf nodded and smiled. "That is one of my specialties."

Domodedovo International Airport
Moscow, Russia

BOLAN AND GRIMALDI stood off to the side in a cramped room as custom officials went through every pocket and crevice of their luggage and equipment, which consisted of a couple of laptops, a camcorder and several cameras. The camcorder case had special compartments for secret pistols and other weaponry, but none was in the case at this time. There was only a large quantity of rubles, euros and US currency for traveling and bribing expenses. Bolan assumed that their weapons had already been delivered to the American Embassy by special diplomatic pouch. In the meantime, both he and Grimaldi stood by patiently and watched the thorough search.

Grimaldi yawned. "Let me know if you find anything. The tooth fairy might've left an extra quarter in there."

The Russian customs agent turned to look at him. "Tooth fairy? Who is that?"

"My BFF," Grimaldi said. "I give him a lot of business knocking guys' teeth out."

The customs agent frowned and went back to his search.

After finding nothing and reviewing both of their passports again, the agents allowed Bolan and Grimaldi to pass through the gate. As they mingled with the crowds moving through the massive airport toward the front entrance and the lines of taxis beyond it, Bolan did quick but comprehensive checks for any prying eyes or ears. Seeing nothing out of the ordinary, he took out his satellite phone and hit the app that detected any listening devices pointed at them. Finding none, he punched in the familiar number as they paused under the sloping archway that separated the main entrance of the airport from the adjacent aisles that contained the lines of taxis.

Brognola answered after the first ring.

"Greetings from Moscow," Bolan said.

"Dobrobih vyeh-cher," Brognola answered. "How was the flight?"

"Uneventful." Bolan glanced at his partner. "Of course, if Jack had been at the controls it would've been a lot smoother and faster."

Grimaldi grinned and shot him a wink.

"I hope he didn't make an ass out of himself complaining to the flight attendants," Brognola said.

"You know better than that," Bolan replied. "Any updates?"

"Everything's still on track, but don't forget to pay your respects at the Embassy."

"Roger that," Bolan said. He knew Brognola was referring to the arrival of their weapons. Both men were used to using a code of sorts, even though the satellite phones contained the most up-to-date encryption devices available. Moreover, Bolan felt his current connection would be more secure than any of the phones at the American Embassy. It had been built by Russian construction crews and contained a myriad of listening devices embedded in every room. It was all part of the ongoing cat-and-mouse game. "Anything else we should know?"

Brognola sighed. "Maybe, maybe not. We just got word that Alexander Grodovich was released from prison."

Bolan searched his memory of recent and past files.

"The millionaire Russian businessman with purported ties to organized crime, right? He got sent up the river a couple of years ago."

"Right. His release, which supposedly involved a presidential pardon, came out of the blue." Brognola laughed. "Although the president must have been feeling magnanimous. He pardoned a few others, too, including those women's rights protestors with the suggestive name. But we're still wondering how this Grodovich thing is going to play out. So since you're in the neighborhood…"

"We'll nose around a bit," Bolan said, glancing at Grimaldi. "I'm sure Jack wants to do some sightseeing."

After promising to check back, Bolan disconnected and they hailed a cab at random. They had a rendezvous to make by twenty-one hundred.

As they got into the cab Grimaldi leaned back in the seat as Bolan gave the driver the address of their hotel. The man nodded and tossed his cigarette out the car window.

"Hey," Grimaldi said as the vehicle took off with a start. "You know who we ought to look up while we're here?"

Bolan said nothing.

"Natalia," Grimaldi said. "What was her last name?'

Bolan knew her last name was Kournikova, but he still said nothing.

"You know who I mean, right?" Grimaldi said. "She owes us, big time, after the way we helped her out in that Caribbean deal." He paused and grinned. "Plus, I think she kinda had the hots for me."

"She did," Bolan said, allowing himself a rare grin. "But only in your dreams."

3

*The Grand International Hotel
Moscow, Russia*

GRODOVICH ADJUSTED HIS white terry cloth robe as he
watched the two prostitutes collect their jackets and head
for the door. As the women left, the redhead winked at
him, but the blonde had a distressed look on her face.

He turned to Mikhal, who had just joined him in the
main room of the suite. The giant still had on his prison
pants and was buttoning his prison shirt. He was wearing his massive prison shoes, as well. Grodovich smiled.

"You have dressed in a hurry," he said.

"I did not bother getting undressed," Mikhal said. "I
am too used to the ways of Krasnoyarsk."

Indeed, Grodovich could smell that Mikhal had not
bothered to bathe yet. The ways of Detention Center 6
were not discarded easily. The only time one risked getting completely undressed was during their weekly shower.
Predators lurked everywhere.

"Did you enjoy yourself?" Grodovich asked.

The giant grinned, the smile stretching over the rocky
unevenness of his dentition.

"There will be plenty of other women," Grodovich

said. "Prettier ones than those. But soon we have to complete our preparations. I must meet with a former business associate."

Mikhal nodded. "When do we leave?"

"As soon as our friend Stieglitz returns with our new clothes and the rest of our equipment."

Mikhal nodded again.

Grodovich heard the door opening and saw Stieglitz enter with several other men. The man immediately behind Stieglitz was the one who caught Grodovich's attention. He was perhaps thirty, with jet-black hair brushed back from his face. His eyes were a brownish-yellow and his body looked powerful under the dark nylon shirt he wore. He moved with a smooth grace, like some feral animal that had been captured but not completely tamed. Grodovich could tell the man had a pistol holstered on the right side of his back and some sort of folding knife clipped inside his pants pocket.

Four other men trailed into the room behind them. Grodovich recognized one of them as the tailor who had been by earlier to take their measurements. Grodovich assumed it would be an easy task to prepare clothing for him, but Mikhal was another matter. The tailor had balked, saying he would have to make a pattern for a man so large. Stieglitz had told him that was fine, so long as he had everything ready by eight o'clock that night. When the tailor had protested, Stieglitz stepped forward and slapped the little man across the face. That shut him up, and Stieglitz had seemed pleased with himself.

At last he'd found someone he wasn't afraid to hit, Grodovich thought. He was already starting to despise the bespectacled, baldheaded little worm. But it was now eight o'clock and the tailor had numerous parcels no doubt containing the clothes. Perhaps Stieglitz had more prestige than Grodovich had thought.

"This is Boris Rovalev," Stieglitz said. "He will be accompanying you on this mission as your bodyguard and personal assistant."

And spy, no doubt, Grodovich thought. The last thing he wanted was a government agent reporting on his every move.

Grodovich shook his head. "I do not need him. I have Mikhal to assist and protect me."

Rovalev smirked. "This clown? Perhaps he could protect you in Krasnoyarsk, but this is the real world."

Mikhal's face twisted into a frown and he stepped forward, his massive body tensing, like a mountain ready to unleash an avalanche.

"You will not speak disrespectfully to me," he said, his childlike voice sounding so out of place. "Or I will hurt you."

Rovalev stepped back and the small pistol was suddenly in his hand. His lips parted in a smile.

"Not that I would need this to stop you," he said. "But you make such an inviting target I can hardly resist."

Stieglitz stepped between them. "Stop this nonsense at once." After glancing at each of the two poised men, he turned to Grodovich. "Have you forgotten where you were little more than twenty-four hours ago?"

Grodovich considered this and then placed a hand on Mikhal's chest, urging him back with gentle pressure. At the same time he faced Rovalev and said, "Put that away. We can all work together."

Rovalev's eyes held those of Mikhal for a few seconds more, then he slipped the pistol back into its holster. He nodded and said, "Another time, perhaps."

Mikhal seemed satisfied with the uneasy truce. He

turned back to Stieglitz and asked, "Do you have our new clothes?"

Stieglitz motioned for the tailor to step forward and said, "Do the giant first." He put his hand in his pocket and withdrew a mobile phone as he walked Grodovich away from the others. "You will now use this to establish contact with your former partner, Yuri Kadyrov."

Grodovich accepted the phone, turning it over in his hand to admire the sleekness of the plastic. He'd been planning to call Yuri soon anyway, but why was Stieglitz pressing the issue? He went through his lexicon of old numbers, trying to recall the one he needed as he turned the phone over and over in his palm.

Stieglitz snorted and shook his head in obvious frustration.

Patience is not his strong suit, Grodovich thought. Or could it be the sign of a man under tremendous pressure?

He decided to test him.

Grodovich made a show of handing the phone back to Stieglitz. "I am sorry, but I can't remember any numbers. It has been too long. They have no doubt been changed anyway."

Stieglitz seemed to become more agitated. "His current number has already been placed into the phone. You need only to consult the memory listing."

Grodovich raised his eyebrows. "And what am I to say to him?"

"Tell him you have been released and you wish to resume your position in your company," Stieglitz said. "Ask him what he has planned." He paused and looked askance at Grodovich. "See if he tells you of the Lumumba negotiation."

"The Lumumba negotiation?"

"An African dictator. Kadyrov is negotiating an arms deal with him. They are scheduled to meet in Antwerp the day after tomorrow. The African is purported to be in possession of a large conflict diamond."

Grodovich nodded. A conflict diamond… So that was it. They needed him to push the illicit gem through the Kimberley Process to launder its dubious origin. But surely Yuri could do that just as easily as he. When he'd gone to prison, Grodovich had left his partner in charge, and it made sense that he would be continuing with the business as usual. It seemed simple enough. There was something more. He could sense it. "What are you not telling me?"

Stieglitz adjusted his gold-rimmed glasses and stared at him. "He intends to betray you, to take over the entire operation himself."

Grodovich shook his head. "Impossible. Yuri and I grew up together. We have been friends all our lives. He would not betray me. Ever."

"He already has."

Grodovich saw a sly smile creep over the other man's lips.

Stieglitz cocked an eyebrow as he canted his head to the left. "Do you remember the day I came to get you in Krasnoyarsk? Those men who attacked you in the stairwell… They were Chechen, were they not?"

Grodovich said nothing. What was this worm implying?

Stieglitz continued, "Who do you think sent them?"

Grodovich had been wondering about that unprovoked attack. Why would Chechens ambush him? Chechens… Like Yuri. It could explain a lot.

"Yuri?" Grodovich said, his voice sounding hoarse. "You're saying he sent them?"

Stieglitz held his gaze and did not speak for several seconds. Finally, after what seemed like an eternity, he answered. "We originally contacted him trying to find out whether he would work with us. But in the end, we determined that he was not to be trusted. Yuri Kadyrov is half Chechen, is he not? Do you know what his name means in his native language?"

"The powerful," Grodovich said, still confused by the possibility of betrayal from his trusted friend. "He used to make a point of telling me that when we were children."

"And since your incarceration he has been in charge of your organization, has he not?"

"Yes, but he has also made sure the monthly bribes were paid to the guards."

"Those same guards who abandoned you in that prison stairwell?" Stieglitz asked. He waited a few moments before adding, "I have already had them interrogated. They confessed. They were bribed by Kadyrov to leave you alone. To let those Chechens butcher you. Upon my arrival, I found out about this plan when I issued a strict order that if you were harmed they would be held personally responsible. I sent another contingent of guards to rescue you. Do you recall this?"

Grodovich thought back. Although it had been Mikhal who rescued him, the second contingent of guards had arrived in a timely fashion. Perhaps this worm Stieglitz was telling the truth. Perhaps Yuri had been behind the attack.

Stieglitz placed a palm on Grodovich's shoulder.

He recoiled.

"So you see," Stieglitz said softly, "there is no one to trust but me, no way to go but forward, as I direct you."

Grodovich slowly nodded. In his mind, however, the question kept repeating: But where is it you wish to take me?

The Blue Sputnik Nightclub
Moscow, Russia

BOLAN AND GRIMALDI sat at a corner table in the smoky semi-darkness, a neon stroboscopic light flashing over the bodies of the gyrating dancers. Bolan kept scanning the room, his drink in his hand, untouched. Grimaldi sat with his left hand propping up his head, his glass on the table in front of them.

"They need to pass a clean air act around here," Grimaldi said. He glared at the man smoking a long cigarette with the hand-crushed filters. "Are we going to wait here all night for this joker to show?"

"It shouldn't be much longer," Bolan said.

"And you know this how?"

"Our friend's been sitting at a table near the other end of the bar for the past thirty-two minutes."

Grimaldi jerked forward. "He has?"

Bolan nodded. Prior to their flight he'd memorized the file photos of the Agency personnel working the transport. Then he'd destroyed them.

"Third table from the far end of the room," Bolan said.

Grimaldi resumed his relaxed posture. "The redheaded dude, smoking the cigarette and making time with the nice-looking babe, right?"

Bolan nodded. The man's name was Donald Framer. Seven years with the Agency, the last four of which had been spent in Europe at various posts. Framer was fluent in five languages, including Russian.

Bolan was getting tired of the waiting, too, but he didn't want to tip Framer's hand. The man was obviously being extra cautious, which, considering the environment, was understandable.

Just then, Framer stood up and, while still addressing the female at his table, pointed toward the men's room. Bolan leaned over to Grimaldi and said, "Keep your eyes open."

Grimaldi gave a slight nod and continued with his affectation of boredom. Bolan knew that in reality little was now escaping his partner's notice.

The washroom was located near the back. Bolan got there first and found it to be occupied by two men who stood there smoking and conversing in Russian. He stopped and stared at both of them, raising an eyebrow, and they quickly left the washroom. After verifying that the two stalls were empty, Bolan went to the long metal trough adjacent to the sinks. Nothing out of the ordinary appeared to have been placed there. He took out his satellite phone, selected the app designed to detect listening devices and did a fast scan. Again, nothing was noted.

The door pushed open and Framer came in, his gaze fixed on Bolan.

"Excuse me," he said in Russian.

"That's okay," Bolan replied in English. "I was just leaving." He looked around. "This place is clean, by the way."

The pungent odor of the water closet made the statement absurd on its surface, but Framer nodded as he walked to the trough and started unzipping his fly. "They say the one in the coffee shop down the block is even better."

Bolan nodded and pushed through the door. He went back to the table and sat next to Grimaldi. "Let's go,"

"About damn time," Grimaldi muttered as he stood. Bolan dropped a few coins on the table for the waitress and headed for the door. The woman who'd been talking to Framer gave them a quick, penetrating look as they passed. She licked her lips.

Both Bolan and Grimaldi ignored her.

Outside the cool late autumn air felt good after the smoky atmosphere inside the club. Grimaldi coughed once as he finished slipping on his jacket and said, "That's a good hour of my life I'll never get back. Where's he meeting us?"

"The coffee shop at the end of the block," Bolan said.

After buying two coffees they took up a position at a table near the entrance. A pair of young lovers was sitting head-to-head at a table toward the back. Aside from the matronly clerk behind the counter, who seemed consumed with trying to count the pastries, no one else was in the place. Bolan had a good view of both the front door and the street through the window. Grimaldi sat opposite him so he could scan the rear of the shop. He took a small sip from his cup and made a face.

"Damn, this stuff's almost as bad as Aaron's brew."

Bolan smiled. "Maybe we can arrange a contest." He kept watching the street as they sat and waited.

Framer took another fifteen minutes to arrive. He strode in with the awkward gait of a semi-intoxicated man without giving them so much as a notice. After ordering himself a cup of coffee and a pastry, he started toward the rear area, did an exaggerated double take when he saw the two lovers and immediately turned around. He shuffled to the table next to Bolan and Grimaldi and plopped down, a simper stretched across his face.

When it was apparent that neither the clerk nor the young couple was paying them any attention, Framer spoke in sotto voce: "You're my two contractors?"

"We are," Bolan said.

He looked at Grimaldi. "You must be Cooper, right?"

"Wrong." Grimaldi pointed to Bolan. "That's Cooper."

"I'm Don Framer."

"Glad you could make it," Grimaldi said.

The smile on Framer's face disappeared as he took another quick glance around, then leaned closer to them.

"Listen," he said. "I don't want any shit from you."

Grimaldi smirked.

Framer stared back at him.

"Let's keep on track," Bolan said. "We're here to assist in any way we can."

Framer inhaled sharply and whispered, "Good, as long as you don't forget I'm in charge and you guys have to do everything I say. Got it?"

Grimaldi snorted. "Listen, sonny—"

Bolan held up a hand. "What's your plan?"

Framer continued to glare at Grimaldi for a few seconds more, then said in a whisper, "Our assets are going to the movies tomorrow night at nineteen hundred. The Rossiya Cinemas." He paused again and glanced around, centering on the two young lovers near the back. "Were they here when you got here?"

Bolan nodded.

Framer continued to study them. The man and woman leaned forward over the table, their foreheads together, their lips occasionally touching.

"Looks like a case of true love to me," Grimaldi said.

"Yeah, well, take it from me," Framer said, "things aren't always what they seem."

Grimaldi frowned and seemed ready to respond, but Bolan shot him a hard look.

"Let's get back to the task at hand, all right?" the Executioner said.

Both Framer and Grimaldi nodded.

"What's the rest of it?" Bolan asked, keeping his voice low. He looked through the large window and saw a woman walking across the street. She was the same one from the bar.

"The abbreviated version is one of my ops is going to bring a car by the rear doors," Framer said, lowering his voice again. "We're going to sneak out at fourteen-twenty-three hours. From there we'll take the long way over to Moscow Station. That's Leningradsky Station to the uninformed. I need you two there no later than sixteen-three-thirty hours. We meet in the shops by the departures section. Have tickets to St. Petersburg on the Red Arrow for everyone. You with me so far?"

"Way ahead of you," Grimaldi said. "You want us to escort them both across the border into Helsinki, right?"

Framer pursed his lips and then nodded. "Think you can handle that? I'll have a team waiting in Petersburg with the false passports. If you take the bullet train you should arrive there in about three and a half hours."

"Sounds like a plan," Bolan said. "Who else knows about it?"

"Huh? Nobody." Framer frowned. "What do you think I am? A goddamn amateur or something?"

Bolan ignored the question. "Who've you got assisting in this?"

Framer shrugged and ran down the list of names, adding, "All agency personnel, by the way."

"You should be operating on the assumption that your plan might have been compromised," Bolan said. "Do you have an alternate?"

"An alternate? Shit. We don't need one," Framer said. He paused, frowned and looked around. When he spoke again his voice was almost inaudible. "I've been stationed here for the past year. I know what I'm doing."

Bolan exchanged a quick glance with Grimaldi.

"What?" Framer asked. "You got a problem?"

Grimaldi started to speak, but Bolan cut him off. "Why don't you go over it again, in detail this time?"

Framer looked at the Executioner, rolled his eyes and began speaking in slow, deliberate tones, giving them a detailed rundown of his plan. "Meet Burns and his friend inside the cinema. All three of the operatives will sit in different rows near the back. One of the team, who will already be inside, will get up halfway through the movie, ostensibly to go to the washroom. Instead he'll text another agent, who'll drive their van to the nearby alley. Burns and his friend will get up, followed by Framer. While the first operative makes a show of buying and then spilling his soft drink in the lobby, Framer and his two charges will sneak down the side aisle to the emergency exit doors that lead to the alley. The operative in the van will be waiting there and they'll all drive away."

He ended with a sarcastic, "Okay?"

"I don't know," Grimaldi said. "Sounds like it's got a couple of weak spots. How do you know they won't stop you in the van before you get to the train station?"

Framer rolled his eyes. "Look, we thought of that, too. We're going to exit the van on the next block and take a taxi to Leningradsky Station."

Grimaldi shook his head. "I still don't like it much."

Before he could say anything else, Framer broke in. "You don't have to. All you two-bit players have to do is get us our tickets. Get it?"

Grimaldi glared at him.

"Why the train?" Bolan asked. "It wouldn't hurt to have a backup plan."

"Yeah," Grimaldi said. "Trains run along the tracks, which are on the ground, meaning they can be stopped along the way. I'm a pilot. I can fly you out."

"Thanks for the physics lesson," Framer said. "And because trains don't fly, we can slip off along the way if we have to and fade into the countryside. I'm fluent in Russian."

"Who was that woman you were talking with back at the nightclub?" Bolan asked.

Framer shrugged. "Just a piece of ass." He glanced at his watch. "I told her I'd be back. Maybe I'll take her up to my place tonight." He winked and grinned a knowing grin. "It helps if you can speak the language."

"Have you known her long?" Bolan asked.

"A couple of weeks. She thinks I'm here on business. She's hot, ain't she?"

"Very," Bolan said. "And she walked by on the other side of the street a few minutes ago. She's probably FSB assigned to watch you."

Framer's grin disappeared and he shook his head, the red in his cheeks almost matching the shade of his hair. "Huh? No way."

Bolan said nothing.

"Listen, pal," Framer continued. "You don't know what you're talking about. I can spot an FSB agent with my eyes closed."

"No, *you* listen, pal," Grimaldi said. "We've been doing this since you were in high school, so when we say something, it would behoove you to shut up and listen."

Framer started to respond, but Bolan cut in. "Okay, we'll go with your plan for now."

Framer pursed his lips and reached into his pocket, withdrawing a small cell phone and setting it on the table. "This is a burner phone. My number's programmed into it."

Bolan tucked the phone into his pocket. "One other thing. I'd strongly suggest that you avoid any contacts with indigenous personnel tonight."

"That means keep it in your pants," Grimaldi said.

Framer got to his feet. "Like I said, I'm no amateur, and you guys are just the backups. Contract employees. I'm running the show, get it?"

Grimaldi started to speak, but another harsh glance from Bolan stopped him. Finally, Framer nodded and headed for the door.

Bolan and Grimaldi watched him open it, step outside and then close it so forcefully the glass in the frame shook.

The woman behind the counter shot them a mean glance.

"Looks like we're overstayed our welcome," Bolan said. "Let's just hope Framer takes our advice about the woman. Otherwise, we're going to be using our special equipment from the embassy sooner rather than later."

"Don't we always?" Grimaldi asked with a grin.

The Grand International Hotel

STIEGLITZ GLANCED AT the clock: three minutes before midnight. He wiped his forehead and continued to wait for the phone call he knew would come. When his mobile phone rang exactly two minutes later, he had it in his hand and immediately answered the call with his customary salutation.

"Is everything set, as far as the plan?" the voice asked.

"Yes, sir," Stieglitz said, maintaining the proper amount of deference in his tone. "I have planted the seeds of distrust in Grodovich, but he sounded very cordial on the phone with Kadyrov."

A few seconds of silence, then: "Good. And what of the other matter? The Americans?"

"I'm having them watched," Stieglitz said. "At a distance, of course. The known operative met with two men believed to be American operatives this evening, first at a nightclub and then at a coffeehouse."

"This is in relation to their planned extraction of their traitor, Burns?"

"Yes, sir." Stieglitz said.

More silence. "Very well. Keep them under surveillance. Let their plan proceed to the designated point. We must find out who else is involved."

"Yes, sir. It will be done. Exactly as you specified."

Stieglitz could hear the other man's sigh.

"Burns has outlived his usefulness. Have the Black Wolf terminate him once we discover the identity of his Russian confederate."

"And the American agents? Should we kill them all, as well?"

"Let me think that over. It would send a good message to the American president not to interfere in our domestic affairs, but we do need to sprinkle enough breadcrumbs that will lead them to Antwerp." His punctuating chuckle sounded low and ominous. "It is an interesting consideration, leaving an opponent's knights on the board for a time in order to set up the ultimate checkmate of his king."

The voice said nothing for several seconds more. Stieglitz could hear the man's breathing. Finally, he spoke again: "This is what you shall do…"

4

American Embassy
Moscow, Russia

BOLAN AND GRIMALDI were in a small private room checking over the weapons that had been delivered via diplomatic pouch. It contained Bolan's Beretta 93R, Grimaldi's .40-caliber SIG Sauer P226, several loaded magazines, two level 3 ballistic vests, two holsters and Bolan's folding Espada knife. They'd be traveling light, but getting caught with anything they couldn't drop and leave would be asking for a free trip to a Siberian prison. As they were finishing their equipment checks, the phone rang.

Bolan and Grimaldi exchanged glances and Bolan picked it up.

"Mr. Cooper?" The female receptionist's voice sounded timid and confused.

Bolan answered in the affirmative.

"Umm," the woman said, "I have a rather unsettling situation here. A messenger just dropped off a note for you."

Bolan had the sudden urge to look out a window and check the street, but the room they were in had no windows.

"It's addressed to me?" he asked.

"Yes, sir. Matt Cooper. That's you, isn't it?"

Matt Cooper was the name on Bolan's passport and the one he usually used when on assignment. The record of him entering the country would be easily traceable, but sending him a message about thirty minutes after he and Grimaldi had entered the Embassy said two things: someone had gone to a lot of trouble to track him down, and they had him under surveillance.

"I'll be right down," he said and hung up.

Grimaldi looked at him. "Trouble?"

Bolan shook his head slowly. "Not sure." He'd assumed they were being watched as soon as they'd touched down in Moscow, and they continually took precautions when moving around. The FSB had far-reaching tentacles and was not hampered by the same restrictions US agencies were. But the audacity of this overt contact was meant to send a message. Big Brother was not only watching—he also wanted to talk.

After retrieving the message, he returned to the security of the windowless room. Grimaldi was in his T-shirt slipping the panels of his vest into the black carrier.

"Fan mail from some flounder?" he asked.

Bolan grabbed latex gloves from a dispenser box on the wall next to the door, slipped them on and examined the envelope carefully, first shaking it gently and then scanning it with his cell phone app that detected chemical agents. Nothing registered. It wasn't standard business size, but rather a much smaller, card-sized lavender envelope. Plus, it reeked of perfume.

Grimaldi stepped closer, waving one hand in front of his nose. "Man, I can smell that from across the damn room." He spread some newspaper pages on top of the table.

Bolan used the thumb-stud to open the blade of his knife, fitted the tip under the lip of the envelope and sliced the top open. The smell of the perfume was stronger as he carefully probed the envelope with the blade of his knife before dumping the contents out. It was a small, colorful card featuring an array of bright flowers on the front with letters in the Cyrillic alphabet. He used the blade to push open the card. The inside had more Cyrillic lettering, under which was a phone number and a handwritten sentence in English:

> *Valenko, in case you have forgotten my number...*
> *Nikita*

The cursive was both elegant and audacious.

"Is that from who I think it's from?" Grimaldi asked.

Bolan nodded. "Natalia Valencia Kournikova. Looks like we'll have to shake whoever is following us and find a couple more burner phones for some quick calls."

The Grand International Hotel

STIEGLITZ WAS SURPRISED at how well Rovalev was getting along with Grodovich. They sat with an unspoken cordiality at a table in the luxurious hotel suite playing chess, each man studying the board intently before making any move. The giant was another matter. The behemoth stood at Grodovich's side, looming over the table. But he and Rovalev seemed to have developed a tacit agreement of sorts.

The Russian Bear and the Black Wolf, Stieglitz thought. Natural enemies. It would be interesting to see which of them prevailed when the time came. But that was a matter for the future.

He snapped his fingers to get their attention.

Neither man looked up from the chessboard.

Irritated, Stieglitz cleared his throat and said directly to Rovalev, "I need to speak with you."

"You may speak," the Black Wolf replied, a glint of a smile showing on his hirsute face.

Grodovich smirked.

Stieglitz said nothing, instead standing there for a few seconds to let his anger become evident. As he reached into his pocket and withdrew his special phone, a gesture meant only to intimidate the Black Wolf, Rovalev used his forefinger to tip over his king and stood.

"You would have checkmate in three moves anyway," the Black Wolf said.

Grodovich smiled benignly, but his eyes shot from Rovalev to Stieglitz. He nodded.

Rovalev stepped away from the table, holding out his hand. "I must see to this matter, but perhaps Mikhal would care to give you a game."

The giant's face remained impassive and he did not move.

"Mikhal does not play chess," Grodovich said. "But perhaps I shall teach him."

As Stieglitz moved out of the suite and into an adjacent room he motioned for the other man to follow. When Rovalev stepped beside him, Stieglitz closed the door.

"What is the status of your operatives?" he asked. "Are they following the Americans?"

Rovalev had a look of utter boredom. "Yes. Burns left his apartment an hour ago and went to the Rossiya Cinemas. He is watching the movie. The operative known as Framer and another of his fellows are also in the cinema. Earlier this morning one member of the CIA group rented a vehicle, a white van. He is currently driving around the Dorogomilovo district. The other two operatives were at the American Embassy this morning until ten o'clock. My surveillance team lost track of them when they went into a heavily populated shopping district. They were last seen entering a store that sells electronic devices."

"What? You lost them?" Stieglitz could feel the veins in his neck tightening.

Rovalev shrugged. "They are apparently supernumeraries. The real quarry is Burns. As long as we continue to track his movements, we will have no trouble locating the traitor and eliminating them all."

Stieglitz pursed his lips. Failure was not an option for him, and even though the American defector and his Russian traitor friend were only a small tear in the fabric of the plan, Stieglitz had to be certain of every detail. There could be no slipups, no loose ends. He told this to Rovalev.

The Black Wolf nodded. The man could be deferential when it suited his purpose.

"I want you to see to this personally," Stieglitz said. His fingers caressed the hard plastic shell of his special phone.

The Black Wolf canted his head slightly to the right and smiled, his white teeth showing through the dark mustache and beard.

"Rest assured, Counselor Stieglitz," he said, "that will not be a problem."

BOLAN TOLD GRIMALDI to set up behind some garbage cans and watch the mouth of the alley. It was fourteen-ten hours and it had taken them longer than they'd expected to shake their Russian surveillance operatives. He squatted next to Grimaldi and took out his satellite phone. Brognola answered on the second ring.

"I hope you're calling with a sitrep," Brognola said.

"That's a rog," Bolan replied. "But we're on the move and it'll have to be quick."

Brognola grunted.

"This may not have a happy ending," Bolan said. "The Agency boy is a bit short on experience and his plan has more holes than a slice of Limburger."

"Great. Can you intercede?"

"It's not looking too good. He's got all the players in his court, and the ball's already in play. Jack and I have been playing catch-up. If we have to, we can try to grab the assets and steal a plane to fly out."

Bolan heard Brognola's long, slow exhale. "Dammit. I was afraid of this. What are the chances you'll be able to break the asset free if things go south?"

"I'd say the chances are slim to none," Bolan said. "You want us to effect a hostile takeover?"

Brognola was silent for a few seconds, then he said, "Only if you absolutely have to. Since you're not there in any official capacity, body checking the Agency would be a hard sell to the President, but I know he wants Burns back in the good old USA. See if you can shore things up, and above all, watch your own asses."

"Is it worth it?" Bolan asked. "If the Russians aren't watching him that closely, it most likely means he's given them all he had to give."

"Good point," Brognola said. "But the propaganda aspect still gives him some value."

"Plus whatever info his friend has," Bolan said.

Grimaldi slapped Bolan's arm. "One of our shadows just showed up."

The Executioner glanced toward the street and saw one of the operatives who'd been following them walk by, his head bobbling like a loose pivot as he looked around.

"Roger that," Bolan said. "We have to go."

"Stay safe," Brognola said.

"We'll do our best." Bolan terminated the call.

"What's the plan?" Grimaldi asked.

Bolan glanced at his watch. Fifteen-twenty. "Let's go get Framer his train tickets."

Grimaldi's mouth twisted into a frown and he shook his head. "I got a real bad feeling about this one," he said.

"You and me both," Bolan replied.

STIEGLITZ WAS FEELING the familiar tugging in his bowels as the car sped through the streets. He sat in the rear. Rovalev sat in the front passenger seat while one of his lackeys drove. The Black Wolf was talking in a low voice on his mobile and Stieglitz wondered what information the man was getting from the operatives he'd assigned to follow Burns and the CIA agents. The pressure of this mission, the entire affair, was crushing Stieglitz like a metal can in a vise. He was not cut out for this type of work. Intelligence work. His mind was better suited for planning and analysis. It was he, after all, who had devised this diamond scheme in the first place. And that was, no doubt, the reason the supreme leader had assigned him to ensure its completion.

"I'm certain that you're up to the task," he'd said. The implication was clear: if you are not, you will be held accountable.

He tapped his fingers on the back of Rovalev's seat. "What is going on? Have they located them yet?"

Rovalev held up his hand and continued talking. Moments later he said something and terminated the call. His white teeth glinted against the dark beard as he turned.

"They are following the white van at this time," he said. "Inside the cinema the Americans met up with another individual. A Russian national. They sat in the same movie for a time, then one of the Americans created a diversion in the lobby while the other three sneaked out a back entrance and entered the van."

"The Americans met with a Russian?" Stieglitz asked.

This man had to be the traitor. He had to know who it was. "Have you identified him?"

The Black Wolf smiled again. "My operatives photographed him. They are emailing a copy to me." He held up his smartphone.

The icon showed a file was in transit.

So close, Stieglitz thought. So close.

Rovalev's phone chimed with the completed photographic transfer. The Black Wolf punched in the code and held the screen toward Stieglitz.

The pear-shaped man in the picture looked startlingly familiar, but Stieglitz had to be sure. "Make it bigger."

Rovalev moved his fingers over the screen, enlarging the photo. The image of the man's face, caught as he turned to look behind him, was unmistakable.

Arkadi Kropotkin.

Stieglitz almost lost control of his bowels, so great was his shock. He'd never suspected his personal assistant, Arkadi, would betray him. Stieglitz swallowed with some difficulty. The Kremlin would hold him responsible for this. Arkadi had been privy to Stieglitz's most private strategy sessions. If the bastard had told the Americans about the diamond plan... But no, he would not. He might have told Burns, but the American traitor would no doubt withhold any key information until he returned to the United States.

The plan is safe, Stieglitz thought. At least for the moment. But it was imperative that Arkadi be apprehended before the Americans could sneak him out of Russia. And why would he be trying to defect with the traitorous American? Seconds later the answer came to him. He knew the American was homosexual... Of course, Arkadi must be one of them, as well. The thought disgusted Stieglitz, but it did make sense. In all the years he'd known Arkadi, the fat little cretin had never once mentioned taking pleasure with a woman.

"Do you know him?" Rovalev asked in a matter-of-fact tone, as if he were conversing about the weather.

"Yes," Stieglitz said. "It's imperative that he be apprehended immediately."

The Black Wolf's mobile chimed again. He withdrew it and pressed some buttons, answering an incoming call. His voice was low. Stieglitz strained to hear what the man was saying.

"A taxi? You are certain?" The Black Wolf turned back to Stieglitz. "They have left the van and entered a taxi. My men are following both of them now."

"Is Arkadi in the cab?" Stieglitz asked. Then he realized that Rovalev was not familiar with their quarry's first name. "The man in the photograph, is he in the taxi?"

The Black Wolf was conversing again on his phone, nodding, talking, laughing.

"Is he in that cab?" Stieglitz demanded.

Rovalev held up his hand and continued to speak. After issuing a few orders he ended the call and turned back to Stieglitz.

"I had to split up my surveillance team," he said. "They appear to be heading north on Sadovaya-Chernogryazs-kaya in the direction of Komsomolskaya Square. It is my guess, if they are seeking to slip out of the country, as your female operative said, they will leave by train. Of the three rail terminals in the Square, Leningradsky is the only one with a bullet train to St. Petersburg."

"They must not be allowed to escape," Stieglitz said. "They must not escape."

"Then let us see that they do not," the Black Wolf replied.

Komsomolskaya Square

BOLAN AND GRIMALDI stood in the shadows of a small restaurant across the boulevard from the large white-and-yellow two-story stone building with the rectangular, centered clock tower. It was sixteen-ten and Framer had texted that they were on their way with an ETA of ten minutes.

Meet us inside the main entrance, the text read.

Bolan showed it to Grimaldi and asked him to text Framer an acknowledgment.

"Sure," Grimaldi said. "And what are you going to do?"

"I've got one more phone call to make," Bolan said as he took out one of the burner phones they'd bought at the electronics store.

Grimaldi smiled. "Nikita?"

Bolan didn't answer. He punched in the number from the message he'd received at the Embassy. It rang several times. He was sure it was a disposable phone. There was no way an FSB agent was going to give him anything else. Finally she answered, her voice seductive. Bolan could visualize the blond hair cascading around her beautiful face.

"Ah, Valenko," she said, using Bolan's alias from long ago. "I was hoping you would call me."

"Did you miss me?" Bolan asked.

Her laugh was musical. "Of course. Just as I miss the Caribbean and our swim."

Bolan remembered their brief encounter. "I do, too."

She laughed again, then her voice turned serious. "Valenko, I felt obligated to contact you. When I saw the surveillance video of you at the Blue Sputnik you looked so handsome. I had hoped you would come to visit me one day."

"Well, here I am."

"Yes, but not to visit me. Just to retrieve someone."

Bolan raised an eyebrow. On that Caribbean island he'd saved her life, and now she was repaying the favor with a warning, at considerable risk to herself and her career. Too many good people were risking their lives on both sides of this to assure the repatriation of a traitor who would no doubt never be held accountable for his actions.

"Valenko," she said. "I must leave you now. I would ask that you come to see me while you are here, but…that would not be wise. Do you understand what I am saying?"

"I do," Bolan said. "*Spasibo* and *do svidaniya*."

He terminated the call, dropped the cell phone to the street and ground it to pieces under his heel.

"So what'd she have to say?" Grimaldi asked.

Bolan felt his mouth tug into a tight line. "It was an informal warning. She was letting me know that they know we're here and why. Exactly why."

"That asshole Framer," Grimaldi said. "He must have spilled his guts to that woman."

"Maybe he talks in his sleep," Bolan said. "Regardless, Natalia was giving us a courtesy warning. They know we're here for Burns, so they've got to be watching him as well as us."

"Which means we've probably got company on the way," Grimaldi said.

Bolan nodded. "We'd better see about that hostile takeover."

5

Leningradsky Station
Moscow, Russia

BOLAN AND GRIMALDI waited just inside a small shop. Both
sides of the main entranceway leading to the departures
and arrivals gates were lined with numerous stores. Two
second-story walkways running the length of the long
room loomed above them on each side—the high ground.
Rays of fading sunlight shone through the windows along
either side of the walkways. It was sixteen-twenty-four
hours.

Bolan kept scanning the crowds of people bustling into
the main hallway. He caught a glimpse of Framer's red hair
first. The Agent was being followed by two other men, one
of whom Bolan recognized as Larry Burns, despite the cap
he'd pulled low on his head. The other was an overweight
man of about forty wearing a gray suit and a hat. A look
of abject fear was stretched across the man's face and his
cheeks jiggled with each rapid step.

Bolan looked to Grimaldi, who nodded that he'd seen
them, too. He stepped out of the store and walked toward
the ungainly trio, motioning fractionally at Framer to go

into the store. Framer caught the gesture and steered the other two men into the shop.

"You have the tickets?" he asked as he stepped close to Bolan.

"I do," Bolan said. "But I think you've been compromised."

"What? What makes you think that?"

"It's complicated. I'd suggest we turn around and get out of here right now."

Framer's mouth twisted into a scowl. "Not unless you give me a damn good reason."

"What the hell's going on?" Burns said. "I thought you had all the bases covered?"

"Blame those asshole defectors who turn over sensitive, confidential data to our enemies for that," Grimaldi said. He stopped and stroked his jaw in an exaggerated fashion. "Oh, wait, you're one of those guys, aren't you?"

Burns puckered his mouth, then opened it, but no sound came out.

Kropotkan pulled at his arm. "Lawrence, what is going on? If they catch me trying to defect, they will kill me and you, as well."

Burns gave a tight smile. "It'll be all right, Arkadi. I promise."

Bolan was growing impatient. He looked directly at Framer. "Look, we can play *Let's Make a Deal* later. Right now we've got a small margin of time to vacate this place. We've got a plane chartered to fly us out of here. We can be in St. Petersburg in an hour."

Framer seemed completely deflated. "Let me think this through," he muttered.

"Think fast," Bolan said.

"Ah, I think the time for thinking's over," Grimaldi said. "Looks like we got company."

Bolan's eyes shot to the front entrance, where half a dozen men burst through the doors. From the bulges under their jackets it was obvious that all of them carried handguns. Two of them remained at the big, arching doors—the only way back toward the front entrance of the station. Another man suddenly appeared on the upper walkway on the opposite side of the room. From inside the shop, Bolan couldn't see if there was another man posted right above them, but he went with that assumption. The gunmen had the high ground and superiority of numbers. The four other men on the lower level began walking down the center of the hallway, then split into twos, each pair systematically inspecting the shops on either side of the room. Bolan estimated that the two on this side would find them in about thirty seconds. They had to move fast.

"Framer, you two head toward the doors leading to the departure gates." Bolan pointed to the Agency man and Burns. "Jack, you take him—" Bolan pointed to Kropotkan "—and make your way down the other side. Let's hope they're looking for a trio and not just two guys. Walk briskly, but don't run. Once you get through those doors go as fast as you can toward the departure tracks. Stay with Jack. He'll lead you out."

"What are you gonna do?" Framer asked.

"Slow them down a tad," Bolan said. "I'll catch up with you on the other side."

"But—" Framer started to say.

"No buts," Grimaldi said, grabbing Kropotkan's collar. "Let's move."

"Don't you manhandle him," Burns said as Framer hustled him toward the door.

What a mess, Bolan thought as he reached inside his jacket and fitted the sound suppressor onto the end of his Beretta 93R. The less noise, the better for this initial encounter. He watched the progress of the four men and saw that one of the interceptors on this side of the room had noticed the departing duos. The man slapped the shoulder of his compatriot and the other man's head swiveled toward Framer and Burns. It made sense that they would be on the lookout for Framer's red hair. He should have given the Agency man a hat. Bolan grabbed a pair of hats from the rack and tossed several rubles to the clerk. As he walked he slipped one of the hats on and picked up a can that appeared to be an assortment of mixed nuts. It was light but would have to do.

STIEGLITZ FELT THE nervousness encroaching on his intestines once again. The Black Wolf was talking on his mobile and gesturing for his lackey to drive faster through the afternoon traffic.

Rovalev turned to him.

"My men have located them," he said. "It was as I predicted. They are in Leningradsky Station. We should have them all in a matter of minutes."

Stieglitz felt a wave of relief, but then the bile rose in his throat. He would not feel safe until he was sure, until he personally watched Rovalev extract every bit of divulged information from the traitor.

"What are you waiting for?" he yelled. "Proceed there at once. I want to see them in custody."

The Black Wolf directed his driver to hurry and Stieglitz was thrown backward into the seat as the vehicle accelerated.

"We will be there soon," Rovalev said, assuming a relaxed posture, even as the car continued to swerve and speed through the busy traffic.

Not soon enough, Stieglitz thought. Not soon enough.

6

Leningradsky Station
Moscow, Russia

As THE EXECUTIONER was stepping to the edge of the store the clerk called out to him. Bolan ignored him and as the clerk yelled again, the head of the first assailant turned in their direction. Bolan threw the can of nuts like he was gunning down a runner trying to steal a base. The can struck the man directly in the nose and he reeled backward, his arms flying, a Tokarev pistol suddenly visible in his hand. The pistol discharged into the air and customers recoiled from the explosion. The second man whirled toward Bolan, his hand reaching under his jacket and emerging with a Tokarev, as well. A woman in the crowd screamed and all at once people were scattering in all directions.

Bolan was approximately twelve feet away from the two men, but he closed the distance quickly. These guys had no compunction about pulling and using their weapons in a crowded, public place, which most likely meant they were either mercenaries or thugs, rather than cops. It also meant they were fair game.

Bolan whipped the extended barrel of the Beretta across the face of the second assailant. He fell to the ground, his Tokarev clattering on the hard concrete. Adjusting his stance, Bolan smashed his left fist into the temple of the other assailant, whose nose was already cut and bleeding from the tossed can of nuts. This man collapsed, as well. Bolan stooped to pick up their pistols and dropped them in a trash can. A round zinged by him. He looked up and saw the man on the second-story walkway in a shooter's stance, using both hands to control his big pistol.

Crouching, Bolan targeted the gunman and squeezed off two shots with the Beretta. The suppressor whispered, accompanied by the metallic clinking of the slide cycling with each round, ejecting the shell casings.

The man on the upper walkway grabbed his chest, the pistol falling from his grasp. He tried to straighten up, then sagged downward, his limp arm jutting out under the barrier and hanging over the edge.

More people screamed and shouted. Bolan heard a pair of shots. The men directly across from him were firing. A woman standing to his left jerked, screamed and fell, the back of her coat showing a crimson hole.

Another shot. Bolan felt the round zipping by his head.

The Executioner brought the Beretta up using a point-shooting technique he'd mastered. This method had been born out of necessity because the sights were obscured by the elevated rim of the sound suppressor.

Bolan squeezed the trigger twice and the first of the two assailants across the way fell. The second grabbed a young man and held him as a human shield. Then the assailant brought his right arm over the squirming youth's shoulder and began firing. The jostling of his hostage threw off his aim and Bolan was able to drop him with a quick head shot.

Five down, at least three more to go, he thought.

He glanced toward the doors leading to the train tracks. There was no sign of Grimaldi and the others. Assuming they'd got through the doors, Bolan made his break. Shots echoed from behind him. Two more people running beside him dropped. Bolan slipped the selector switch to full auto and angled toward his right. Above, he caught a glimpse of a man running along the upper walkway, a big semi-automatic pistol in his right hand. The man's eyes locked on Bolan and he brought the weapon to the ready position.

The Executioner sent a 3-round burst upward and the man danced away from the edge of the walkway. Another round whizzed by and Bolan saw two more assailants approaching from the doors. One of them was firing a pistol and the other was talking on a cell phone.

Looks like their reinforcements are coming, Bolan thought as he continued his zigzagging run toward the doors leading to the tracks. It was too risky to send another 3-round burst at the shooters on this level. Too many innocent civilians around.

Bolan burst through the doors, pushing as many people down as he could. Their best chance would be to stay on the ground until the shooting stopped. Several of them shouted in Russian, got back up and continued their scattered running.

Bolan scanned the departure area. It was a long open-ended enclosure with dozens of train engines butting up to the platforms. Overhead sodium vapor lights illuminated the cavernous interior, and the smell of diesel oil hung in the air.

Someone waved off to his right.

Grimaldi.

Bolan ran toward him.

Grimaldi motioned for Bolan to keep coming as he ducked behind a large, motorized luggage truck. As Bolan got there he saw the other three men, Framer, Burns and Kropotkan, crouching behind the metal shell. Burns and

Kropotkan looked sick. Framer held a small Walther PPK6 in his right hand.

"How many playmates we up against?" Grimaldi asked, his SIG Sauer P226 leveled across the seat of the luggage cart. He hadn't bothered with a sound suppressor.

"Three left in there," Bolan said, gesturing toward the doors he'd just come through. "But one of them looked to be calling in reinforcements."

"This is all my fault," Framer said.

"It is," Burns shouted. "You promised you'd keep us safe. You lied to us."

"Lawrence, what are we going to do?" Kropotkan sobbed.

"Calm down," Bolan said. He glanced around and then tapped Grimaldi on the shoulder. "Think you can hotwire that cart behind us?"

"Of course," Grimaldi said, as he moved toward the adjacent cart.

"What are we going to do?" Framer asked.

"Get ready to jump on that cart once Jack gets it going," Bolan said.

Suddenly five men burst through the doors. One of them held a Skorpion machine-pistol. He began firing indiscriminately in all directions. People were screaming, and the man with the Skorpion smiled when a woman pointed toward the luggage cart Bolan and the others were behind.

Milliseconds later, rounds from the machine-pistol peppered the metallic framework of the cart like a blast of hailstones. Another burst from the Skorpion sent more rounds skidding along the concrete platform underneath the wheels of the cart. Framer grunted and grabbed at his calf.

Bolan shot the man twice. The slide on his Beretta was not yet locked back, but he knew he would soon be close to an empty magazine. He had two more full mags in the pouch on his belt, but he couldn't afford to waste any rounds.

More bullets sank into the metal skin of the cart.

Burns had the look of pure panic on his face as he started to get up.

"Stay down," Bolan said, seeing the man's movement peripherally, while still trying to engage the other assailants.

But Burns stood and began running. Kropotkan did the same. Framer tried grabbing at one of them but missed.

A new volley of exploding rounds sounded and Kropotkan's legs suddenly seemed to slow to a deliberate stutter step. He gripped his belly and rolled forward, twisting and squirming on the ground.

"Got it," Grimaldi yelled and he waved them over.

Burns turned and yelled at Kropotkan, then seeing him on the ground, stopped and stood there. Several rounds ripped into his chest. Bolan motioned for Framer to go to Grimaldi. The Agency man's mouth was tugged into a thin, tight line, but he nodded and began half-running, half-crawling toward the second cart.

Bolan edged over the cart's seat and began firing to give them cover. The Beretta continued its metallic chinking sound until the slide locked back, signaling the magazine was empty. One of the attackers had fallen and the other two had ducked out of sight. Doing a combat reload, Bolan ran to Burns as Grimaldi provided cover. The man's breath was ragged and flecks of blood were aspirating with every gasp. Frothy patches of red bubbles were emanating from the holes in his torso with each breath.

Sucking chest wounds, Bolan thought, looking for something to seal the wounds. He reached into his left pants pocket and took out the train tickets. As he tore open the front of the man's bloody shirt, Burns reached up and encircled Bolan's neck with both of his hands.

Burns attempted to pull the Executioner downward but instead lifted his own body upward, his mouth next to Bolan's left ear.

"Arkadi?" he managed to say.

Bolan pushed Burns away, and then looked at the man's lover. Kropotkan stared back with unblinking eyes canted slightly downward. Blood streamed from both his nose and mouth. It didn't look good.

"I'll check him in a second," Bolan said. "Let me take care of you first."

Burns coughed, spraying Bolan's face with blood. The Executioner recoiled as he was once again grabbed by the dying man.

"He's dead, isn't he?" Burns said.

Bolan didn't answer. He brought his palm up to push the dying man away as gently as he could.

"And so am I," Burns said, his voice a hollow whisper. "Listen, Grodovich... Diamonds... Hot rocks... Rad—"

Burns sagged toward the concrete floor, his eyes fixed in a blank stare.

Bolan checked for a pulse and any other signs of life. Nothing.

He moved to Kropotkan and repeated the action. The man was dead.

Bolan flattened as a fresh burst of rounds bounced off the concrete a few yards away. He brought the Beretta around and perused the field of fire. He saw two sets of feet crouching behind a luggage cart by the door and another man leaning a bit too far out from behind a train engine. Bolan shot that man first and then lowered his Beretta to almost floor level and fired a quick burst at the exposed sets of feet.

As the trio of assailants fell, Bolan was up and moving. Grimaldi was helping Framer onto the idling luggage cart. The lower portion of Framer's right pant leg was sodden with blood.

"Are they dead?" he asked.

Bolan nodded.

"Man, I really messed up, didn't I?" Framer said. His face was twisted with pain.

Bolan hopped on the cart and told Grimaldi to head for the end of the platform.

"I hope they aren't flanking us," Grimaldi said.

"We'll know shortly," Bolan replied, scanning the rear and then the area in front of them. The cart whisked along, but it wasn't nearly fast enough to suit Bolan. He figured an all-out sprint would have been faster, but not while carrying a wounded man.

"You guys leave me here," Framer said through gritted teeth. "I can try to hold them off."

"No one gets left behind," Bolan said.

The end of the platform was thirty feet away. They had covered the distance expeditiously, but Bolan caught sight of five new assailants running toward them from the doors.

"More company," Bolan said as he brought the Beretta up and sent two 3-round bursts toward the approaching foes. They all dodged to the side and about five seconds later began returning fire.

Grimaldi twisted the wheel, causing the cart to lurch into a sudden skid. The vehicle slid sideways for several feet, then came to a stop about three feet from the barrier at the end of the platform.

"Where to, boss?" Grimaldi asked.

Bolan did a quick assessment. The large wall separating the tracks from the outside streets was perhaps one hundred yards long. If they could get to the end, their chances of getting up onto the street would be pretty good.

Another round zipped by them and Bolan told Grimaldi and Framer to make a break for the end of the wall.

"I'll catch up to you," Bolan said, crouching behind the cart and aiming his Beretta toward the advancing assailants.

"I should do that," Framer said.

"Worry about being a hero later," Grimaldi said. "Come on."

Framer shook his head. "I don't think I can make it. My leg hurts too bad."

"Well, why didn't you say so?" Grimaldi asked as he grabbed Framer and helped him to the edge of the platform. Grimaldi jumped down and then dragged Framer off the platform, shouldering the man in piggyback fashion. "See you at the other end," he called to Bolan.

The Executioner waited.

STIEGLITZ GRIPPED THE back of the driver's seat with both hands, so violent were the vehicle's jerking movements as Rovalev's idiot driver wound through the streets toward Komsomolskaya Square.

"Are we almost there?" Stieglitz yelled.

Seconds later the question was answered for him as Leningradsky Station became visible.

Rovalev, who was busy talking on his cell phone, glanced back at him and lifted his hand. He listened and then shouted some instructions to the driver. The man swerved away from the curb.

"The Americans are heading for the street," Rovalev said, taking out a huge pistol.

"The American defector and the Russian traitor must

not escape," Stieglitz said. "They must not. Do you understand?"

The Black Wolf merely glanced back at him with one of his feral smiles.

7

Outside Leningradsky Station

BOLAN FOLLOWED GRIMALDI, who was making pretty good progress toward the end of the long concrete wall that provided shelter for the parked trains. Beyond it the blue sky was a pastel background for a smattering of leafless trees.

The row of trees was set next to a smaller concrete wall perhaps thirty feet high. Dry, dead grass hung over the uppermost edge and beyond that was the concrete and asphalt of Komsomolskaya Square. Getting up the face of that sheer, thirty-foot wall presented a new problem. The tracks gradually rose to street level, but the incremental elevation added an additional three hundred yards to the distance they had to cover. Grimaldi was visibly slowing. If they were going to make it, they'd have to speed things up.

Bolan scanned the station platform. Still no sign of any bad guys. He turned and sprinted up to Grimaldi and touched his arm.

"I'll spell you," Bolan said and waited while Grimaldi came to a stop and lowered Framer to the ground.

"Okay by me," Grimaldi said, his breath coming in sharp gasps as he fumbled for his gun.

Bolan handed him the Beretta 93R. "Here. Use mine."

Grimaldi's eyes widened and a grin stretched across his face. "Hot damn. You mean you're letting me hold the baby?"

"And shoot it, too," Bolan said, shifting Framer onto his back. He set off at as fast a pace as he could manage carrying the additional one hundred-ninety pounds. The ground was uneven, full of ruts and dips and loose gravel. Bolan heard the sharp, metallic sound of the Beretta firing and knew Grimaldi must have acquired some targets.

Bolan began to run with a renewed sense of urgency. Suddenly, off to his left he saw something that looked like a life preserver on a stormy sea: metal rungs in the side of the concrete wall, forming a ladder leading to the street.

"Jack," Bolan called. "Look."

Grimaldi fired off two more rounds and glanced over his right shoulder. His grin seemed to get larger.

Bolan got to the ladder and pulled on the first rung, testing its sturdiness. It seemed tight. He backed into the wall, taking some of Framer's weight off his legs. Grimaldi was at his side now. Bolan noticed the Beretta's slide was locked back. He grabbed the weapon, dropped the magazine and inserted a new one. Turning his head slightly he addressed Framer.

"Our only chance is to get up this ladder to the street. Think you can make it?"

Framer's breathing was almost as heavy as Grimaldi's. He shook his head. "Leave me here. I'm too weak."

The man's face was grayish. They had to get him medical attention soon, very soon. Bolan motioned for Grimaldi to go up first.

"I'll bring him up while you do cover fire," Bolan said. "Be ready to help me lift him when we get near the top."

Without another word Grimaldi quickly began scaling the iron rungs.

Bolan saw movement about fifty yards away, then a pinpoint muzzle flash. Wherever the round went, it didn't seem to be close to them. A shot from that distance with a handgun would be challenging. Rather than return useless fire, he waited.

Seconds later Grimaldi called down to him: "Clear up here so far."

Holstering the Beretta, the Executioner turned back to Framer. "Listen," Bolan said. "I'm going to climb up the ladder. You've got to hold on to me with all you've got. Ready?"

Framer grunted a yes.

Bolan waited for the man to secure his grip, then began climbing. The extra weight made every movement difficult, but the soldier continued the rigorous ascent.

When they were halfway up, Bolan tried to count the number of rungs to the top. Perhaps fifteen more. Fifteen, fourteen, thirteen—

The iron rung under his left hand popped loose from its concrete socket.

Framer screamed.

Bolan managed to tighten his grip on the other rung he was still holding, avoiding the deadly plunge.

Lucky thirteen, he thought, readjusting his grip and reaching for the next rung.

He hoped there were no more loose ones.

Eleven.

Ten.

Nine.

"I was gonna tell you about that loose rung," Grimaldi yelled down at them. He fired off three more rounds with his SIG.

When Bolan finally reached the top he could feel the sweat cascading from his face like a waterfall.

He bellied over the sharp concrete edge then rolled slightly, pushing Framer onto a patch of grass.

Perhaps forty feet beyond them, through a mixture of high grass and scrawny trees, he could see cars driving by.

"Let's see if we can commandeer a cab out of here," he said.

Grimaldi flashed a quick smile. "I'm all for that."

"Wait," Framer said through clenched teeth. "The rest of my team should be just down the block in the van." Struggling, he pulled out his cell phone and punched in a number. After a few more seconds he spoke. "We're just north of the station on the street. Get here quick. I'm hit." Framer listened, then replaced the phone in his pocket. "They're on their way."

Grimaldi fired another shot over the lip of the abutment and said, "So are the bad guys."

"Come on," Bolan said, picking up Framer and heading through the tall grass toward the street.

As the vehicle pulled up in front of Leningradsky Station, Stieglitz could hardly contain his anxiety. He leaned forward and grabbed Rovalev's arm. It felt like iron. The Black Wolf shot back a quick, searing look and Stieglitz removed his hand, feeling a bit lightheaded. This was becoming a nightmare. If the plan was revealed prematurely, it would be a disaster, not only for him, but for the country, as well.

I am not cut out for this, he thought. But the Kremlin knows. That is why they assigned the Black Wolf to assist me.

Rovalev yelled at the driver to start proceeding with caution along the curb. He pointed toward the far end of the station.

"Where are we going?" Stieglitz asked. "I thought your men had them trapped?"

The Black Wolf didn't answer. He kept skimming the crowds walking along the sidewalk. At the main entrance people seemed to be flooding out, running toward the sidewalk.

"What is going on?" Stieglitz demanded.

"I told you," Rovalev said, his voiçe the epitome of serenity. "The Americans are heading for the street."

Did that mean they had escaped Rovalev's men?

"Where are they now?" Stieglitz asked. "Is the Russian traitor with them?"

Rovalev held up his hand again, as if he were threatening to slap a recalcitrant child.

Stieglitz was about to say something else when the Black Wolf pointed and said, "The white van. There it is. Follow it."

"THAT'S IT," FRAMER SAID. "There."

Bolan saw the white GAZelle heading toward them. He picked up Framer again, slinging the injured man over his shoulder like a sack of potatoes, then jogged toward the curb. Grimaldi was right behind them.

The van had almost gone completely by, but Bolan managed to break through the dense shrubbery in time to wave at the driver. The GAZelle came to a screeching halt as it pulled over to the curb. Several cars were trapped behind it and began honking their horns.

Great, Bolan thought. Nothing like a little noise to attract some attention.

Grimaldi raced around them and pulled open the side door. He jumped into the rear of the van as Bolan stopped and set Framer down as easily as he could. They needed to get to the triage room at the American Embassy, where they had a physician and nurse on staff. Framer had lost a lot of blood and needed immediate treatment, but he could probably survive. Grimaldi echoed Bolan's thoughts by yelling, "Your partner's shot. Get us to the Embassy ASAP, and don't spare the horses."

Framer hissed in pain as his injured leg hit the ground.

"Sorry," Bolan said, "but we've got to move fast."

"I know. Thanks," Framer said. "You guys saved my life."

Bolan started to reply when Framer's head jerked like he'd been poleaxed. The sound of the shot mixed with the spray of blood from the temple wound as his head twisted violently.

Bolan pushed him inside the van as he withdrew his Beretta, flipping the selector switch to burst mode. He saw a wiry-looking man with dark hair and a beard pointing a pistol at them from about forty yards away. Bolan fired a quick burst and the man flattened.

The Executioner jumped inside the van and yelled, "Take off. We have company."

The van lurched forward and Bolan went to the rear doors. The back windows gave him a clear view of the traffic behind them. He leaned against the wall of vehicle and did a quick weapon assessment, estimating his magazine was now at least half empty.

"Jack, how many rounds you got?" he asked.

Grimaldi was laying Framer's head onto the floor of the van. From the nature of the wound and the limpness of the man's body, Bolan figured the shot had been fatal. Grimaldi shook his head, then pulled out his SIG Sauer, dropping the magazine.

"Two rounds left in this mag and eight more here." He patted the other magazine in the pouch on his belt.

Bolan nodded and checked the traffic to the rear again. It looked pretty standard except for a blue four-door Lada Niva that was coming up on them fast. The guy with the black hair and beard was in the front passenger seat starting to lean out of an open window. The big, semi-automatic pistol was in his right hand.

Bolan detached the sound suppressor from the Berretta and held it against the rear window with his left hand. He made sure that his right index finger was outside the trigger guard and then struck the sound suppressor with the edge of his right hand. The glass splintered. Most of it was still in place except for a hole along the bottom where the sound suppressor had fractured the glass.

The Executioner flipped the selector switch to single shot mode and took aim at the front of the Lada Niva. He put the first round through the driver's side of the windshield and fired a second round next to the first. The vehicle immediately began to slow and Bolan fired three more rounds, placing two at radiator level in the grill and the final one into the left front tire as the Lada Niva curved to the right and smashed into another vehicle in the adjacent lane.

Bolan caught a glimpse of the guy with the dark beard. The Executioner was expecting rage, but he saw none. In fact, the man seemed to be smiling.

He scanned the rest of the traffic behind them but saw nothing to make him suspect that any of the other mercenaries or the police were following them. He doubted the crew of mercs would call the police, but that didn't mean someone else hadn't.

"Slow it down a bit, but get us there soon," Bolan said to the driver.

The man glanced over his shoulder. "How's Framer doing?"

"He didn't make it," Grimaldi said, reaching over and closing the dead man's eyes.

8

The Diamond Quarter
Antwerp, Belgium

GRODOVICH WATCHED THE video as it played out on the tablet. Black-and-white images of four men dressed in black rushing around a jewelry store smashing displays and grabbing the contents.

Yuri Kadyrov stood next to him, the man's pungent body odor reminding Grodovich of his time behind prison walls. Lots of smelly, rough, unpleasant men ready to lash out at the slightest provocation. Mikhal's looming presence next to him, as well as the suave Rovalev, the Black Wolf, gave Grodovich a slight feeling of solace. But still twelve armed men, all loyal to Kadyrov, sat across from them at the big wooden table in the well-lit office, smoking and drinking. Several of their weapons sat on the tabletop. This close, the Robie Cats looked as lethal as Grodovich remembered them to be. Yet they seemed relaxed, almost nonthreatening, at least for the moment.

Yuri passed some gas and poured himself another drink. His swarthy face was wet with perspiration and his large, unkempt mustache had copious droplets of vodka hanging on the ends of the dark hairs.

The man is essentially a modern barbarian, Grodovich thought. Like the hordes that had swept over the country-side raping and pillaging in centuries past. Was it really on his order that those Chechens attacked me in the stairwell?

Kadyrov laughed and pointed to the screen. "Now listen to this part."

The sound of the news reporter's voice overlaid the video of the dark silhouettes.

"This group, known as the Robie Cats," the reporter said, giving the last name a French inflection, "are one of the most notorious jewel thieves in Europe. Believed to be responsible for over a dozen high-profile robberies in Germany, England, Italy and Switzerland, they take their name from the character played by Cary Grant in the classic Alfred Hitchcock thriller *To Catch a Thief.*"

Kadyrov paused the video, laughed again and continued, speaking in heavily accented English. "The guy is full of shit. We never called ourselves anything. The Robies was something the fucking reporters came up with. Who even remembers that old movie now?" He downed the remainder of his glass of vodka. "But who can complain, eh? We made it to *60 Minutes*, the biggest American news show." He stopped and poured more vodka into Grodovich's glass and then his own. "Drink, my brother. We must celebrate your release. Tell me, how did you manage it?"

"It was not easy," Grodovich said. He smiled and brought the glass to his lips, although he only sipped the clear liquid. He could feel the tangy burn on his tongue, but as delicious as it was, tonight was not the time to drink. "You will be getting the payment request shortly."

Kadyrov laughed again. Grodovich could tell the man was getting seriously drunk. Was this a sign of nervousness or elation?

Certainly, my return means Yuri will be taking less of

the organization's profits, Grodovich thought, but he had kept the monthly security payments going to the prison guards as well as Mikhal's mother. It had been a constant drain, and perhaps Yuri had grown tired of it. Money would seem a logical motive to order the murder of one's imprisoned partner. In the West, they called it a hostile takeover. In Russia, in the *mafiya*, it was called a necessary business decision.

"You have done well during the time I was away," Grodovich said, looking around the sumptuous office. Stieglitz had been explicit in his instructions: "Reestablish contact with Kadyrov, and tell him you wish to reacquaint yourself with the business but gradually. Be cordial, not demanding. But remember, he has already arranged once for your death."

The words kept echoing inside Grodovich's head, like Raskolnikov in *Crime and Punishment*.

"I'm glad you came here," Kadyrov said, smiling. "But did you have to tell those reporters of your plans? I have a business deal I am working on."

"Ah," Grodovich said. "What kind of deal is it and with whom?" He looked at Kadyrov, trying to monitor his reaction. "I am very eager to resume an active role on our organization. Gradually, of course."

Kadyrov returned the pensive stare, as if he were debating all the possible responses. Then his face twisted into a sly smile and he pointed to Mikhal and Rovalev.

"And you have brought your new friends with you, too, eh?" He grinned. "A mountain and a mountain wolf." He laughed so hard at his own joke that it turned into a coughing jag.

He was back to being good old friendly Yuri—a loveable buffoon fond of strong vodka and beautiful women but as deadly as an Asian cobra once the snake charmer's tune had ended.

After he stopped coughing, Kadyrov took another drink, this one directly from the bottle, belched, got up and walked to a nearby filing cabinet. He set the bottle on top of it, glanced around the room and then removed a picture that was hanging on the wall next to the cabinet, revealing a wall safe. He set the picture on the floor and leaned forward, twisting the dial in different directions. After that he attempted to open the safe, but it remained locked. Kadyrov swore and spun the dial again, this time with a touch of anger, but the safe still would not open.

"Perhaps you have had too much vodka, Yuri," Grodovich said. "Do you want me to assist you?"

Kadyrov snarled a negative reply and leaned closer to the metallic surface, this time twisting the dial with a slow precision. The door popped open and he withdrew a leather case about the size of a large hardcover book. He motioned for Grodovich to join him. Grodovich set his own glass down and stood. As he walked over Mikhal trailed close behind him.

Kadyrov glanced up at the giant as they approached and laughed. "Ah, the mountain comes to Muhammad. Does your big friend follow you everywhere?"

Grodovich nodded and slapped Mikhal's massive shoulder. "I owe him my life. Just the other day, when I was in prison, some men tried to kill me. Mikhal stopped them."

"A dangerous place, prison, eh?" Kadyrov raised his eyebrows and smiled. "And a good companion is like a trusted weapon." He patted his side, where he had a large Tokarev pistol holstered. "But you are done with all that now." He glanced around again as he unzipped the case and parted the folds. A thick sheaf of brown envelopes lined the interior.

Grodovich shot him a questioning look. Kadyrov smiled and removed one of the envelopes. He pulled open the top flap and dumped the contents into his big palm.

A brilliantly fashioned white gold necklace with a serpentine chain lay there, coiled like a sleeping asp. The multifaceted stones glimmered like stars, even in the dim light.

"From our latest acquisition," Kadyrov said softly. "And tomorrow we will be getting more."

So I've heard, Grodovich thought. "Magnificent," he said. "Tell me, are you still using the old Jew to make the adjustments?"

Kadyrov nodded. "Bloom is the best." He carefully returned the necklace to the envelope, sealed it and then replaced it in the case. "It seems a pity to remove them from their comfortable places of residence, eh?" He laughed, picked up the bottle and took another drink. "But nothing is forever."

"Except diamonds," Grodovich said.

Kadyrov laughed again as he took out a long cigarette, pinched the extended filter twice and then struck an affected pose.

"Tell me," Kadyrov said, "do I not look like one of those fucking American movie stars?"

Grodovich looked at him, wondering how much longer he could afford to allow his former partner to live. "Absolutely. Just like Cary Grant."

"Shit," Kadyrov snorted as he stuck the cigarette into his mouth and lit it. "He is dead."

And so are you, Grodovich thought. Only you do not know it yet.

BOLAN WATCHED AS Grimaldi pulled the Citroën into the makeshift parking space on the edge of the ring road. The spot afforded them a glimpse of the tall buildings of the city across the river. Grimaldi shoved the gear shift into reverse and shut off the engine. He released the clutch and then pulled the emergency brake. When he saw Bolan's watchful gaze, he grinned.

"Just making sure," Grimaldi said. "I never quite trust any of these French models, be they plane, train or automobile."

"Are you saying you're prejudiced against French models?" Bolan asked with a smile as he took out his satellite phone.

"Unless they look like Brigitte Bardot." Grimaldi stretched and looked through the windshield at the city below them. "What's this town's major claim to fame again?"

"It's the site of the largest estuary in Western Europe," Bolan said.

"Smells like swamp water and oil refineries to me," Grimaldi said.

"It's got several of those, too," Bolan said as he punched in the number for Stony Man Farm.

"And diamonds," Grimaldi said. "Don't forget about the primary reason we're here."

Brognola answered on the third ring. His voice sounded rusty with sleep.

"Don't tell me I woke you up," Bolan said, placing the phone on speaker so Grimaldi could listen.

"Don't worry about it," Brognola answered, sounding more alert now. "You guys in Antwerp?"

"On the outskirts," Bolan said. "You got any updates for us?"

Brognola sighed. "Yeah, the President was less than pleased about the way things turned out in Moscow. And that's putting it mildly."

"Then he should have let us run the whole show from the get-go," Grimaldi chimed in.

Bolan shot him a quick glance that silenced him.

"My feelings exactly," Brognola said. "But at least we don't have to worry about Burns leaking any more secrets to the Russians." Bolan heard the other man's heavy sigh. "Run his last words by me again, will you?"

Bolan searched his memory, recalling the dying man's last gasping breaths.

"Okay, he said, 'And so am I,' meaning he obviously knew he was dying. Then he added, 'Listen, Grodovich… Diamonds… Hot rocks… Rad—'"

"Rad?" Brognola said. "What the hell did he mean by that?"

"I'm not sure."

"Yeah, me either. Anyway, the parts about Grodovich and the diamonds make sense." Brognola paused to cough. "I told you before about him getting released from prison, right? A Presidential pardon, no less." He coughed again. "Hot rocks…"

"His past association with the Russian *mafiya* fits with the 'hot rocks' statement," Bolan said. "And as for the report of him going to Antwerp, he could be planning on unloading some of his stolen jewels. I'm sure he's got a stockpile. Maybe that's how Grodovich bought his freedom."

"With the sanctions still in place and their economy in the toilet," Brognola said, "the Russian government could probably use an influx of quick cash. And I'm sure that Presidential pardon didn't come cheap. Question is, would it be enough? I mean, even if Grodovich and his boys have a substantial stockpile, it's got to be relatively small potatoes compared to a GNP in trouble and a growing national debt."

"A riddle wrapped in a mystery inside an enigma," Bolan said.

Brognola laughed. "It sure the hell is, Mr. Churchill. Listen, while you and Jack were sneaking out of Russia, Aaron and I did a little digging. Before he left the mother country, Grodovich told a bunch of reporters he was heading to Antwerp to renew ties with some old business acquaintances and that he also planned to make some kind of big announcement shortly."

"Any idea what that might be?"

"I'm not given to rash speculation, but in the meantime, I'd say he's going to unload some of his stolen stockpile in Antwerp."

Bolan considered this. "That's what's been bothering me. If he's planning on dealing with stolen merchandise, why would he be announcing his movements? It'd make more sense to keep a low profile. It almost seems like he wants the attention."

"Yeah, that bothers me, too," Brognola said. "But keep in mind he's been cooped up in a Russian prison for a while. Maybe he just wants to enjoy being back in the limelight."

Bolan said nothing.

"One of his old associates is Yuri Kadyrov," Brognola said. "He's purported to be the head of a group of international jewel thieves called the Robie Cats."

Bolan had heard of the group, as famous for their military precision as their daring and flamboyance.

"Kadyrov's half Russian, half Chechen," Brognola said. "The majority of the Robies are said to be Chechen or Russian mercs, all of whom have extensive combat experience."

"From what I saw in a news program, they looked like they had the moves."

"And how. So you and Jack watch yourselves if you tangle with them." Brognola was silent for a few seconds.

"We've arranged a new cover for you. You guys are Department of Justice agents, as usual, but this time you're investigating stolen jewels from a couple of robberies that occurred in the Diamond District in Manhattan. I'll be emailing you all the info."

Bolan detected a hesitancy in Brognola's tone and knew that the other shoe was about to drop. "What else?"

Brognola laughed. "I'm going to have to work on my poker voice. You're right, there is something else. You'll be tagging up with INTERPOL on this investigation."

Bolan didn't like the thought of being constrained by the international police agency. He was too used to working outside the rules. He thought about protesting but decided against it. Obviously, Brognola and the Bear had gone to substantial trouble to set up this new cover. The least they could do was try to make it work.

"Did you hear me all right?" Brognola finally asked. "I said, you'll be working in conjunction with INTERPOL."

"We heard," Grimaldi said. "But that doesn't mean we have to applaud."

Brognola laughed again. "That's more like it. Now the agent assigned to assist you is named François Lupin. He works out of Paris, but he's en route to Belgium now. Supposed to be an expert on the Robies. I'll email you his contact information. He's expecting your call. Meet with him ASAP, and get busy figuring out what our favorite Russian and his Robie buddies are up to."

"Roger that," Bolan said. But his thoughts were still back in Russia, thinking about the guy with the black beard who'd shot Framer. Bolan wished he'd stayed behind to settle the score.

STIEGLITZ SAT ALONE in the Russian Embassy waiting for his mobile to ring. He'd called as soon as they'd all reached

Antwerp and was told to proceed to the embassy and await further instructions. Although the tumult in his bowels had somewhat subsided, the knot of tension was still present. The enormous hand had only partially loosened its constant grip.

He looked again at the mobile, which was lying on the center of the table. Then, his eyes drifted to the tightly wrapped package that sat a few centimeters from the phone. It had been delivered earlier by diplomatic pouch and was about the size of a man's fist. Stieglitz was certain that Grodovich's lackey, the giant, could palm the item without notice, but in a regular man's hand it would be conspicuous. Like trying to hide a ripe apple or orange in one's pants pocket.

Suddenly, the mobile lit up with an incoming call. He grabbed for it, but his hands were so wet from perspiration that it slipped from his grasp and clattered to the floor.

Oh, please, Stieglitz prayed, do not let it break.

He was in luck. It continued to function normally as he flipped it open and pressed the button to answer the call. The LCD screen listed the caller as BLOCKED, but Stieglitz knew who it was. Only one other person had the number of this special mobile.

"Yes, sir," Stieglitz said, as respectfully as he could.

Silence, then, "Why did it take you so long to answer? What are you doing?"

Stieglitz felt the absence of saliva in his mouth. His throat was dry as well, and he hoped it wouldn't lend a hoarse quality to his voice. He wanted a drink of water but hadn't wanted to risk leaving the privacy of this room for a trip to the facilities.

"I am sorry, sir," he said. "My apologies. I accidentally dropped the mobile."

A few more seconds of silence during which Stieglitz

felt the big hand begin to tighten its grip once more. Then the voice on the other end spoke again. "Very well. Is everything proceeding according to the schedule?"

"Yes, sir. Everything is on time."

"On time… I must tell you, I have never cared for that expression. It sounds so frivolous."

"I am sorry, sir," Stieglitz said. "I will no longer utilize it."

"Are you now in the secured room, as I instructed?"

"Yes, sir."

"And no one else is present?"

"No one, sir."

"And did you take possession of the stone?"

"It is here, sir. Right next to me."

Silence, then, "Who else knows it was synthetically produced?"

This question stunned Stieglitz. No one knew outside the small circle of planners in the Kremlin. Why had he even asked? Then the answer became apparent: Arkadi. News of his intended defection had gotten back to the uppermost echelons of government.

"No one, other than the original inventors of the plan, those who assisted you, has been informed," Stieglitz said. "We had a traitor in our midst, as I'm sure your excellency knows, but he was dealt with accordingly. All is safe. All aspects of the plan are proceeding with the utmost precision." He emitted a nervous half laugh. "A brilliant plan, sir, if I may say so."

Silence. Stieglitz felt the sweat forming under his arms and dripping down his sides. Had he said the wrong thing? Had his obsequiousness been too obvious? He wished to elaborate, to assure that he meant no disrespect, but he dared not speak, lest he say the wrong words. If he had not done so already.

Finally, the voice said, "The incident at Moscow Station was a debacle. I expected the situation to be handled with more circumspection."

"Those were Rovalev's men, sir," Stieglitz said quickly. "I have already reprimanded him for his lack of supervision and scrutiny as well as the recklessness of his subordinates. He has assured me it will not happen again."

Stieglitz felt more sweat forming. The hand inside his gut began to squeeze tighter.

Finally, the voice spoke: "Do you know how to tell the difference between a winner and a loser?"

What is he talking about now? Stieglitz racked his brain for a proper response. Winners and losers? "Do you mean aside from the obvious declaration?"

"If there is no declaration. If it is not readily apparent."

Stieglitz felt the sweat pouring down his face, as if a washer woman had wrung a dirty handkerchief over his bald head. But he had to respond. "No, sir."

"A winner takes responsibility for the actions of all his subordinates, whether good or bad. A loser seeks to pass the blame onto others."

Stieglitz realized to whom he was referring. "Yes, sir. I understand, sir."

"Do you?" The voice was redolent with anger, then went back to its calm but ominous tone. "I am not interested in hearing excuses. Explain this to Rovalev. There will be no more failures. None. This plan must be carried out with the utmost precision. It is as delicate as maneuvering pieces on a chessboard. Now, tell me again that you understand and that there will be no more slipups." His tone was clipped, authoritative, foreboding.

Stieglitz repeated the reassurance.

"Again," the voice said.

Stieglitz obeyed the command.

"Say it again."

He did.

When he'd finished, he waited for more instructions but heard nothing. Tentatively, he spoke into the phone but received no reply and realized the connection had been terminated on the other end.

It had been a lesson in obedience, like training and re-training a dog.

A dog, Stieglitz thought. Is that what I have become?

He carefully closed the mobile, replaced it in his pocket and looked at the wrapped package. Dare he touch it? So many lives hung in the balance, including his own. He had to force himself to reach out, lift the package and place it in his pocket.

It was lighter than he expected, but then again, its substance was more symbolic than material. It had been designed to weigh in at just under three hundred and thirty carets, which was slightly greater than the fabled Congolese Giant.

9

Vlaeykensgang District
Antwerp, Belgium

Two young women, both dressed in fashionably short skirts and tight blouses, strolled into the café, flashing Bolan and Grimaldi a pair of coquettish smiles.

"I'll take the blonde," Grimaldi said, waving to them.

"Take it easy," Bolan said. "We've already got a rendezvous set up, remember?"

"How could I forget? You keep reminding me." Grimaldi frowned slightly. "But I'll bet this François guy isn't going to be half as good-looking as those two."

The young women ordered something from the lady behind the counter. The redhead glanced over her shoulder, blinked and then giggled into her girlfriend's ear. The blonde gave them a furtive glance, as well.

"Let's hope he's dressed more conservatively than they are," Bolan said.

He had been mildly surprised at the warm reception Lupin had given him on the phone. Despite the lateness of the hour, the INTERPOL agent had suggested meeting at a small coffee shop in the Vlaeykensgang District, a cloistered collection of old houses and cobbled courtyards harkening back to the Middle Ages.

"Anyway," Bolan continued, "a little while ago you were complaining that you were tired."

"Hell, I am. I mean, I did most of the driving today." Grimaldi glanced at the two young women again. "But I'm never too tired for romance."

Bolan couldn't help but smile at that. As they sat in the dimly lighted shop drinking mugs of hot chocolate, Bolan reflected on lost opportunities and the image of the bearded assailant's smile when they locked eyes.

Another time, Bolan thought. Another place.

"You're thinking about the shootout, aren't you?" Grimaldi asked.

Bolan said nothing, but his partner seemed to read his mind.

"Yeah, me, too. Sure would've been nice to save that guy Framer." Grimaldi clucked sympathetically. "I didn't much care for him at first, but he had balls. Kind of short in the brains and listening departments, but balls."

The two women turned and moved toward the door, the blonde carrying a paper bag. The redhead jiggled her fingers in a small wave as they passed Bolan and Grimaldi and said something in Flemish that Bolan guessed was flirtatious.

He made no effort to respond.

As they got to the door it suddenly opened and a tall, dark complexioned man stood there. He bowed and made a sweeping gesture for the women to exit before him. After a quick duet of thank-yous from the women, the man smiled broadly and watched their backsides as they passed him. He was broad shouldered and his thick nose looked like it had been broken more than once. After glancing around the shop and seeing no one else, he nodded to Bolan and Grimaldi.

"Ah," the man said in English, his words tinctured with a French accent. "A lovely evening for some coffee, *n'est-ce pas*?"

"But we're drinking hot chocolate," Bolan said, repeating the prearranged meeting signal.

"Tres bien," the man said. He smiled, showing a flash of white teeth. "I shall get some myself."

He moved to the counter and made his purchase, chatting with the server in Flemish. After receiving his drink, the man strode back to their table and stopped, taking a careful sip.

"Ahh," he said. "An excellent suggestion, *messieurs* May I join you?"

"As long as your name is François Lupin," Bolan said.

The man's face suddenly acquired a puzzled look. He reached into his inside jacket pocket and withdrew a black wallet. He flipped it open and looked at it intently for a few seconds, then his mouth stretched into a broad grin.

"Oui, that is what my identification card says." He held the open wallet toward them, displaying a gold-colored badge and an INTERPOL identification card. Then he laughed.

Bolan studied the open badge case, verifying the name and picture.

Lupin flipped the wallet closed and replaced it in his pocket.

"Let me guess," he said. "You are Monsieur Cooper?"

Bolan nodded.

"How'd you know that?" Grimaldi asked.

Lupin turned to him. "I could tell you I am a clairvoyant, but that would be a bit of a lie. I must confess, I recognized your voice from our brief conversation on the telephone."

"Speaking of conversations," Bolan said, "your English is flawless. How many languages do you speak?"

Lupin shrugged. "You are too kind. My father was French, my mother Russian, and I grew up here in Flanders. I picked up those languages growing up, and I learned English because I worked at the ski resorts as an instructor during the latter part of my youth, and I know Spanish because I have an affection for dark haired *señoritas*." He shrugged again, in a self-effacing sort of way. "Eventually, I found my calling in government work as a humble, but vastly underpaid, civil servant. I was assigned to INTERPOL due to my fluency in so many languages."

"Impressive," Bolan said.

Lupin smiled, showing white, evenly spaced teeth. "I have been told that you are here tracing *mes amis*, the Robie Cats. Is that correct?"

"Possibly," Bolan said. "We're also tracking a Russian national named Alexander Grodovich. He just arrived here from Moscow."

Lupin nodded and took a sip from his mug. "I am very familiar with Monsieur Grodovich. Until recently, he was confined in a Russian prison. Two separate prisons, to be exact. His crimes were supposed to be of a financial nature, which does not surprise me. He and his associate, another Russian named Yuri Kadyrov, were partners in an international jewel smuggling ring. For some inexplicable reason, Grodovich was given a pardon and has now returned to Antwerp."

"Any idea what he's planning?" Bolan asked.

Lupin shook his head, drank more hot chocolate and lifted his right eyebrow. "I'm sure it has something to do with diamonds. After all, we are in the diamond capital of the world."

"Before Grodovich left Russia, he held a press conference about entering the international diamond scene again," Bolan said.

"Oui, c'est vrai." He smiled again. "Forgive me, I sometimes slip back into the language of my birth. Grodovich has also met with Kadyrov, who is apparently expecting an important visitor." He paused and studied their faces. "Have you ever heard of Jonathan Lumumba?"

The name struck a chord with Bolan. "He's the leader of one of the rebel factions in the Congo."

Lupin lifted his eyebrow once again and nodded. "Very good, *monsie*—" He paused. "This is getting a bit cumbersome. How is it you wish me to call you?"

"Cooper's fine."

Lupin looked to Grimaldi, who shrugged.

"Your associate is a man of few words, eh?" Lupin said.

"Not really," Bolan replied.

"Yeah," Grimaldi said. "Usually, it's the other way around. I have trouble keeping my mouth shut."

Lupin laughed. "Then it is settled. You may refer to me as François, and I shall call you Cooper, like the American cowboy movie star, and you will be Jacques, like Jacques Cousteau. It is good, *n'est-ce pas?*"

"Fine by us," Bolan said, "but tell us more about Lumumba and how he relates to Grodovich."

Lupin had just finished taking another drink from his mug. He swallowed and nodded. "Lumumba, or *Le Grand Prince*, as he wishes to be called, arrived yesterday from Africa. His previous trips to Europe have all been to obtain funds for the purchase of arms."

"And his currency is diamonds," Bolan said. "Given

the state of the country he's from, we're most likely talking about conflict diamonds."

"Exactly," Lupin said. "It should be noted that this time he has four associates who traveled with him. Three are his bodyguards. Although our customs officials found nothing out of the ordinary in any of their luggage, it is believed he brought with him an undisclosed amount of blood diamonds."

"How'd he do it?" Grimaldi asked.

"Ah, Jacques," Lupin said with a grin. "You can speak after all."

Grimaldi snorted.

Lupin placed his elbows on the table and hunched toward them, lowering his voice. "The fourth individual Lumumba brought with him… The first thing they did upon their arrival at their hotel was to summon a surgeon. It is my strong belief that this fourth individual is most likely a mule. It is believed he has the diamonds concealed internally. In his colon."

Grimaldi grimaced. "I'm sorry I asked."

The right side of Lupin's mouth rose into a half smile. "It should also be of particular interest that the second thing *Le Gran Prince* did upon his arrival was to notify Yuri Kadyrov that he was there. I believe they will set up a meeting as soon as possible. Perhaps for tomorrow evening. It is a meeting I intend to scrupulously monitor."

"Sounds like something we'd like to be in on, as well," Bolan said.

Lupin looked at each of them and winked. "That is exactly what I hoped you would say."

The Van de Roovaart Hotel
Antwerp, Belgium

STIEGLITZ PAUSED AT the edge of the lavish dining room and saw the group of them sitting at one of the large tables.

Grodovich sat at the head, with his faithful giant next to him. Rovalev sat on the opposite side, situated so he had an unimpeded view of the entrance.

A prudent decision for a professional assassin, Stieglitz thought.

He cleared his throat as he stood there, almost obscured by the plush curtain that had been draped over the entrance way.

Rovalev's eyes immediately shot his way.

Grodovich and the giant roared with laughter as a pretty girl bent over their table refilling their wineglasses. No glass sat in front of Rovalev.

Stieglitz cocked his head slightly and moved toward the elevators. By the time he'd gotten to the lifts and pushed the button, the Black Wolf was beside him.

"What is the source of such amusement?" Stieglitz asked, motioning toward the dining room.

"Alexander was relating how Mikhal had his first encounter with a woman a few days ago," Rovalev said.

Stieglitz frowned. So now it was Alexander and Mikhal… He hoped a friendship had not developed between them and Rovalev. It could prove difficult later on. But the Black Wolf's face showed no mirth as he spoke. He looked like a man describing the weather.

The elevator doors opened and Stieglitz and Rovalev stepped inside.

As soon as the doors had closed, Stieglitz spoke in a clipped tone. "Your assignment is not to befriend them."

"You needn't remind me of my assignment," Rovalev said in an equally blasé tone. "Nor of my responsibilities."

The elevator doors opened to their floor. Stieglitz hurriedly stepped into the hallway, withdrawing his key as he glanced around. No one else was there. He motioned for Rovalev to come with him.

Once inside the room, Stieglitz secured the safety lock and then checked thoroughly for anyone else's presence.

"I told you I swept all our rooms earlier for listening devices," Rovalev said. "Do you wish me to repeat the search?"

Stieglitz nodded vigorously. He sat down on the bed and watched the Black Wolf check the room with some attachment he affixed to his mobile. These elaborate espionage games were wearing thin.

I am not intended for such things, he reminded himself.

Finally, Rovalev put his mobile away and said it was all clear.

Stieglitz stood and looked the other man in the eyes.

"What I am about to tell you does not leave this room," he said. "Understood?"

Rovalev nodded, his expression serious, intense.

"The American agents," Stieglitz said, "the same ones who were in Moscow, are here in Antwerp."

"Do you wish me to kill them?"

"No, no," Stieglitz said. "Not at this time. They are being monitored. What was your assessment of the Chechen?"

"Grodovich's partner? A clever fellow. He covers his intelligence with a guise of boorish drunkenness. I suspect he was less inebriated than he pretended to be."

"Do you foresee any problems in killing him and his group of thieves?"

Rovalev shook his head. "He is but a Chechen fox. I am a Russian wolf."

Stieglitz took a deep breath, then exhaled. "It must be done at tomorrow's meeting. Grodovich already knows this will happen. There will be no objection or interference on his part. He believes that Kadyrov sent some men to kill him when he was in prison."

Rovalev raised his right eyebrow. "An assumption we wish him to keep?"

Stieglitz nodded. "You must also kill the man Kadyrov and Grodovich are going to meet. An African named Lumumba. He will have three armed guards with him."

Rovalev nodded again.

"And most important," Stieglitz said, reaching into his coat pocket. His fingers brushed the wrapped package. Did he dare touch it? He did not wish to, but he had no choice. Gripping it, he brought the package out and set it carefully on the middle of the bed. "You must place this on the dead African's body. Make it look as if he had it secreted on him when he arrived."

Rovalev's eyes narrowed. "What is it?"

Stieglitz took another deep breath. How much should he divulge at this time? He'd been ordered to tell Rovalev as much as he needed to know to carry out this phase of the plan—but not everything. Not yet.

Slowly, with trembling fingers, he began to unwrap the package. He had difficulty untying the string wrapped around the box. A knife suddenly appeared in the Black Wolf's hand and with a deft flick of his wrist he severed the troublesome constriction.

Stieglitz recoiled at the sight of the shiny blade. Pursing his lips, he opened the box and removed a wrapped item about the size of an apple. His fingers peeled back the surrounding paper until an uneven, grayish stone was exposed.

"Is that what I think it is?" Rovalev asked.

"A diamond," Stieglitz said, nodding. "A very special diamond." He looked up with as much gravity as he could muster. "One that will change the world."

10

The Diamond Quarter
Antwerp, Belgium

BOLAN AND GRIMALDI sat in the backseat of Lupin's vehicle, a nondescript, black Citroën, and waited while the INTERPOL agent talked on his cell phone. He was in the front passenger seat and another man, whom neither Bolan nor Grimaldi had seen prior to this evening's surveillance, was behind the wheel. One of the benefits of working with INTERPOL, Brognola had told him, was that they could tap into local law enforcement resources without any red tape.

Bolan hadn't been surprised when Lupin came by the hotel to pick them up, advising that the special team was already assembled and monitoring Lumumba's cell phone transmissions.

"You're tapping his line?" Grimaldi asked.

"Of course." Lupin turned in the seat and looked at them. "At the moment we are also triangulating his location." He shook his head. "We are certain he's meeting with the Robies and Monsieur Grodovich, but we do not know where, as of yet. I have two cars following them."

"How many men does he have with him?" Bolan asked.

"Alas, only three," Lupin said. "When our sources at the

hotel advised us of their departure, they also mentioned that Le Gran Prince and his party refused, in a most adamant fashion, any type of services from the maids." He grinned. "That, coupled with them summoning the physician to the hotel, suggests something is amiss in his suite."

"You guys hit it?" Grimaldi asked.

Lupin laughed. "Ah, you Americans. Cowboys all of you. Here in Europe we operate on a less flamboyant *modus operandi*."

"It'd be nice to know if he brought conflict diamonds into the country," Bolan said. "And if he did, whether or not he's got them with him."

"*Mon ami*, I said that we operated with less flamboyance." Lupin smiled. "But I did not say with less resourcefulness. We had a female police officer, masquerading as a maid, enter the suite a few minutes ago."

"And?" Grimaldi said.

Lupin shook his head, a tinge of sadness in his voice. "She found one of the Africans in a very bad way, bleeding profusely from the abdominal area. Internally, as well. He was rushed to the hospital by ambulance."

"The one you said was the mule?" Bolan asked.

Lupin nodded. "From the amount of blood on the bed, it appears that surgery was done in the suite and not with much regard for the comfort or safety of the patient. Unfortunately, the man speaks only some obscure, African tribal language and attempts to question him have proved fruitless."

"That should still be enough to bring Lumumba in for questioning," Bolan said. "But it'll be more solid if you can tie him to Kadyrov."

"And perhaps," Lupin said, "to your target, Monsieur Grodovich, as well." Then his cell phone rang and he held up his finger as he answered it, fitting an earpiece into place. He spoke in Flemish, a language Bolan recognized but did not understand. He and Grimaldi exchanged glances, the message clear between them: it was always difficult to sit in the backseat when you were used to being the driver in the race.

Lupin terminated his conversation and turned in his seat once more.

"They have entered the Diamond Quarter," he said. "They're on De Keyserlei. They are driving with less speed now, and Lumumba is making another phone call. As soon as they stop, we should have their position and be ready to move in."

"How far away are we?" Bolan asked.

Lupin made a clucking sound. "Unfortunately, we are a little ways away, but I have my two men on him. They will watch where Le Gran Prince goes and advise. Do not fear, *mon ami*. We will get them."

Bolan nodded and looked out the window. Night had descended over the city and despite the plethora of lights twinkling in the darkness, something was gnawing at him.

"Of course," Lupin said, "we intend to bring Lumumba in for questioning about the injured man in his hotel room, but unless we find direct evidence of smuggling the conflict diamonds, it will be difficult to arrest the two Russians, as well."

"That's fine," Bolan said. "You take Lumumba and leave us to have a little private conversation with Grodovich and Kadyrov."

"If they remain," Lupin said. "Keep in mind that the Diamantwijk is only a few kilometers from Berchem Airport. Perhaps, if they feel threatened, they will attempt to flee."

"I don't think so," Bolan said "Grodovich made too much of a show before he left Moscow about this big deal he had in the works. I don't think he's going to leave without something to show for his visit."

Lupin's body visibly stiffened as he pressed a button on his cell phone and a finger against the earpiece. Shaking his head, he said something and then turned to them. "The reception is bad. I must get out."

He opened the door and took several long steps away from the car. The conversation lasted about a minute, then Lupin paused, looked at his phone and pressed more buttons. After a moment he started speaking again. This conversation was fairly short, and after a few more minutes, he got back in the car and said something to the local policeman in Flemish and the man shifted into gear. The car started moving forward and accelerated to a fairly fast speed. Lupin turned back to them once more, a broad smile stretched across his face.

"They have stopped," he said. "An old, abandoned factory building near the outer edge of the district. That is, as you Americans say, the good news."

"What's the bad news?" Bolan asked.

"It is a very large building and in a state of disrepair. Scheduled to be rehabilitated." Lupin began punching in more numbers on his cell phone. "I am afraid I must summon more men to assist us before we attempt to enter. After all, I am only a humble civil servant. My pay is not sufficient that I should risk my life."

As he fingered the earpiece again and started talking on the phone, Bolan exchanged a nod with Grimaldi. He knew they were both thinking the same thing: Just get us there and you can wait in the car for your backup. Leave the entry to us.

GRODOVICH FELT A small bit of comfort that Mikhal was at his side as Yuri Kadyrov led them through the hallways

of the huge, abandoned factory, accompanied by two of
his diamond-stealing assistants. One of them held a flashlight and a radio; the other lugged a heavy suitcase filled
with euros and American dollars. After receiving the call
from Lumumba, Yuri told the Robies to spread out, stationing two men at the back entrance and two more just
inside the doors.

Stieglitz had elected to remain at the hotel, saying he
had stomach problems. Grodovich suspected the man was
afraid of the pending trouble. He also knew that Rovalev
and his cohorts were nearby. Stieglitz's plan did not allow
for any treacherous partnerships, especially with thieves.
The Black Wolf would settle all accounts tonight, including revenge for the botched assassination attempt that Yuri
had engineered back at Krasnoyarsk. Rovalev had promised that Mikhal could handle it personally.

For now, his old partner was back to being good old
friendly Yuri, laughing through an affected inebriated
haze. As they walked through the darkness, their path illuminated by flashlights, Grodovich wondered if Stieglitz
was correct. That perhaps Yuri had orchestrated another
assassination for this meeting or maybe shortly thereaf-
ter. Grodovich was gambling with his own life here, so
knowing that the Black Wolf, and his paid mercenaries,
were lurking somewhere close was another way of hedg-
ing his bets.

They were deep inside the bowels of this large structure now. Grodovich could see that the brick walls had
been well built, but little else remained to herald the once
proud construction efforts. The interior held skeletons of
different rooms, some, but not all, of which had walls. The
Robie Cat leading the procession paused and held up his
hand. He lifted a small radio to his mouth and spoke into it.

In Chechen, not Russian.

Yuri and the two Robies accompanying them were the only ones who understood that language. Perhaps his erstwhile partner did indeed have more in mind than a diamond deal with this African butcher.

"Go through here," Yuri said, pointing down a hallway. It was a perfect place for an ambush.

"This is like a maze," he said. "Why are we having this meeting in such a place?"

Yuri smiled. It was more of a leering grin. He'd been slurping up borscht and vodka all afternoon and Grodovich wondered how the man could walk straight.

"Does that concern you, Alexander?" Yuri said and then laughed. "But of course. Prison has made you more cautious. Here, my man and I will go first. And your giant can bring up the rear. You will be well protected."

Mikhal straightened at the mention of him, glaring down at Yuri, who laughed.

"Does your big friend ever smile?" he asked. "I must tell him the legend of Antwerp harbor. It involves a giant who thought he was invincible but ended up getting his hand chopped off before being thrown into the water." Yuri's hand shot out and slapped against Mikhal's huge abdomen. "Tell me, my huge man-mountain, can you swim?"

Mikhal said nothing. He kept glaring at the other man.

One of Yuri's henchman led the way down the corridor while the other left them. Grodovich could hear the muffled sound of an engine of some sort. Then he saw a flicker of light ahead as a door opened. More light shone from the room. A generator must be somewhere nearby.

The man held the door open and they stepped inside. The room was illuminated by three stationary pole lamps, each with a bright electrical bulb glowing from under thin translucent shades. An old wooden table sat in the middle of the floor, with two chairs on either side.

Three black men, wearing dark business suits, white shirts and black neckties and looking very much like professional soldiers, stood behind an immense man who was seated in one of the chairs. This man wore a bright green jacket and a red beret. To say he was big was not to compare him to the likes of Mikhal. Indeed, this man's corpulent form had the look of overindulgence and dissipation rather than strength and power. But although his body appeared soft, his eyes had a cruel, hard cast.

"Jonathan," Yuri said, stepping forward with a wide grin. "How are you, my friend?"

Lumumba smiled but remained seated. A briefcase sat on the floor next to him.

"I am ready to make a deal," the African said and laughed. It had an almost musical quality, dancing up a few octaves and then down again before ending abruptly. Grodovich thought it bore a strange resemblance to the cackling of a madman.

"Then let us not waste time," Yuri said. He motioned for the assisting Robie to place the suitcase on the table. "Let me see the stones."

The African didn't move. Instead, his eyes flickered to Grodovich and then Mikhal. "And who are these others?"

Yuri smiled and placed his left arm around Grodovich's shoulders. "This is my partner, Alexander. He and I grew up on the streets of Moscow, and we've been together ever since." He paused and turned his face toward Grodovich. His breath smelled sweet. "Except for the time he was in prison."

Lumumba's eyes flicked back and forth. He looked like a crocodile eyeing his next meal. "And why have I not seen him before?"

Yuri first squeezed Grodovich's shoulders, then shook him. "As I said, this man here, he just was released from prison, where, I might add, he made no mention of any past associations or business dealings."

Grodovich could almost feel Lumumba's eyes probing him. After perhaps twenty silent seconds, the African snapped his fingers. One of the suited men reached down, picked up the briefcase and set it on the table. Lumumba adjusted the combination locks and flipped the case open. Sheaves of manila envelopes were lined up. Grodovich could see what appeared to be smears of bloody fingerprints on the paper envelopes.

"All quality stones of the utmost merit and repute," Lumumba said. "Do you wish to examine them all?"

Yuri sat in the chair opposite the African and plucked one of the envelopes from the middle of the pack. "These are rough diamonds, I assume?"

The African nodded.

Yuri removed a knife from his pocket and flicked his wrist. The blade popped to an open, locked position. He slid the blade under the lip of the envelope and sliced through the paper, the sharpened edge making a purring sound. After finishing the cut, Yuri slammed the tip of the knife into the tabletop, where it quivered in an upright position.

He poured the contents of the envelope into his open palm. The stones varied in size and color; most were grayish and misshapen. Yuri reached into his pocket, removed a jeweler's loupe and held it to his right eye. One by one, he studied the stones. His face twisted into a frown.

"Are they all of this quality?" he asked.

Lumumba sat there staring at him. Finally, he extended his hand toward the array of envelopes. "See for yourself. As I told you, they are all there and of excellent quality."

As Yuri reached for another envelope, Grodovich felt his mobile phone vibrate inside his pants pocket. It was the signal. Rovalev was here. He strained his ears for the slightest sound and thought he heard a sharp, metallic clinking.

A silencer?

A sharp thump on the wall was followed by the crash of the door being kicked open. Rovalev entered holding a Tokarev pistol with a long sound suppressor attached to the end of the barrel, his arm extended. The nonbearded part of his face was streaked with black stripes, making him look like a wild animal, and a pair of night vision goggles were flipped up on his head. Before anyone could react, Rovalev shot the three African bodyguards, then the Robies standing closest to him. The four men seemed to crumple to the floor in successive order. All of them had been shot in the head.

Rovalev was followed by two more men, who immediately trained their pistols, also equipped with the long silencers, on Yuri and Lumumba.

"I could not help but overhear your last comment," Rovalev said with a smile. His white teeth looked feral in contrast to his black beard and darkened face. "But did you forget to mention the new Congolese giant gem that you have?"

Lumumba's brow furrowed and his head made a slight jerking motion. "Do you know who I am?"

Yuri looked around, too. "That's right. Do you have any idea who you're fucking with, you piece of shit?"

Rovalev swept the barrel of his pistol across Yuri's face. He fell forward slightly and made a grab for the knife.

Mikhal lunged forward with astonishing speed, grabbing both of Yuri's arms and forcing them flat onto the table. Rovalev nodded in an appraising way and then grabbed Yuri's knife with his left hand. As Mikhal kept Yuri's arms immobile, Rovalev rammed the tip of the knife through the back of Yuri's hand with such force that it was pinned to the table. Yuri grunted in pain and yelled, "Alexander, help me."

Grodovich stood there assessing the situation. Whatever pity he may have felt was overwhelmed by the surge of anger when he remembered his terror as the three Chechens cornered him in the prison stairwell.

"Did you really think you could get rid of me so easily when I was in Krasnoyarsk, Yuri?" Grodovich asked in a soft voice.

"What the hell are you talking about?" Yuri managed to say through clenched teeth. The blood was welling up the sides of the blade, running over the olive skin of his hand and onto the tabletop. Soon it would permeate the manila envelopes.

"You betrayed me," Grodovich said, "so you will die now, but as a tribute to our long-ago friendship, I have told Mikhal to make it quick."

"What are you—"

Mikhal's huge hands gripped Yuri's head and neck. The giant's arms and shoulders rolled in opposite directions, accompanied by a face-twisting grimace.

Grodovich heard a brief scream of pain and then a dull snap. Yuri's face suddenly lost all signs of life and his head bobbled loosely on his shoulders as Mikhal released him.

Across the table Lumumba's eyes were opened wide. He did not move as Rovalev rammed the end of the pistol into his mouth and forced him backward. His rotund body dropped on the floor. Rovalev followed, straddling the man, still holding the pistol in Lumumba's mouth. The red beret fell off his head.

"Where is the big gem?" Rovalev asked, his voice low and visceral. "The conflict diamond. The large stone. I know you have it."

Lumumba tried to say something, his words muffled by the metal sound suppressor.

"Where is it, you son of a bitch?" Rovalev yelled. His left hand moved over the dictator's body, then he stopped. "Well, what is this?"

Rovalev withdrew a wrapped item about the size of a small apple from the inside pocket of Lumumba's jacket and held it in front of the man's face.

"Is this it?" Rovalev asked.

Lumumba tried to work his lips and tongue, but the sound was garbled.

"I thought as much," Rovalev said. The Tokarev jerked with subdued explosiveness and an expended casing popped upward and bounced on the hard floor. The African's entire body stiffened. His eyes remained open, but they became unfocused and a puddle of blood formed on the floor beneath his head. Rovalev got to his feet, stepped over the dead man and moved toward Grodovich. He held out the wrapped item.

"The bastard had this in his pocket the entire time," Rovalev said. "Open it."

Grodovich took the item and slowly unwrapped it. Inside was the largest rough diamond he had ever seen. It had to be well over three hundred carets. It would be worth a fortune once it had been polished and cut. He glanced back at Rovalev.

"How did you know?" Grodovich asked.

Rovalev shook his head. "Stieglitz told me. Now, we must leave immediately. The police are on the way."

"But is it safe?" Grodovich asked. "Yuri had several guards—"

"They have been taken care of," Rovalev said. "Come. Now."

Grodovich started to hand the diamond back to him, but the other man shook his head.

"It's your headache now." His white teeth gleamed and he nodded toward the dead African. "Let us hope it brings you more luck than its previous owner."

As THE CITROËN sped through the dark streets, Lupin seemed agitated. He tried to make several phone calls and then popped the earpiece loose and swiveled back to face them.

"My surveillance team does not answer," he said. "I have tried numerous times." His forehead showed rows of creases. "I am hoping it is merely a bad connection."

"Can you reach them by radio?" Bolan asked.

Lupin shook his head. "I ordered that no radios be used. The Robies have excellent frequency scanning equipment." He held up his cell phone. "Mobiles are better."

"How far away are we?" Bolan asked.

"Almost there." Lupin replaced the earpiece and tried another call. He listened, then shook his head.

The local police officer said something in Flemish and Lupin nodded. "That is their car up ahead. Parked."

The driver shut off the headlights and slowly positioned the Citroën behind the dark van. Lupin exited the car immediately and ran to the other vehicle's passenger side. Bolan and Grimaldi got out, as well. Lupin shone his flashlight into the van and stopped.

"Merde," he said, his face showing a look of shock.

The front windows on both sides of the car had been shattered. Bolan swept his flashlight over the interior of the van. Two plainclothes police officers were slumped against their respective doors, each with a bullet to the temple. As Bolan pulled open the front passenger door to check the man for signs of life, the body started to tumble out of the vehicle. Bolan caught him and gently pushed him back on the seat. No pulse.

Grimaldi had moved around to the driver's side door. He opened it, removed his left glove and placed his fingers against the driver's neck. Seconds later he looked at Bolan and shook his head.

"Like Moscow all over again," Grimaldi whispered.

Bolan shone his light over the ground and spotted a shell casing—9 mm, from the look of it. Probably two assailants, one on each side, had crept up to the windows and fired a shot into each man. Quick and neat, like snuffing out two candles at the same time.

"Which building did Grodovich go in?" Bolan asked.

Lupin didn't answer at first. He just kept looking at the car.

Bolan was about to repeat the question, but Lupin said, "That old factory there."

Bolan nodded to Grimaldi, who slipped his glove back on and pulled his SIG Sauer out of its holster. Bolan withdrew his Beretta and they started moving down the street toward the factory.

"Wait," Lupin said. He strode back to the policeman in the Citroën and leaned over, speaking to the man. After a few sentences had been exchanged, Lupin straightened, withdrew a small pistol from a shoulder holster and ran back to Bolan and Grimaldi.

"The other units are still a few minutes away," he said.

"Well, if you think we're going to wait for the cavalry," Grimaldi said, "you haven't seen any John Wayne movies."

"We can't wait," Bolan said. "We're going in."

Lupin placed a palm on Bolan's arm. The Executioner glanced at him, and the INTERPOL man realized the touch was a mistake and withdrew his hand.

"Sorry, *mon ami*," he said. "But I merely wish to say

that I am coming with you. Our local assistant will wait here and direct the rest of the arriving officers."

"Let's go then," Bolan said.

"Those men," Lupin said, his voice cracking a bit. "They were my responsibility. I would prefer to be the first to enter the building. I owe them that much."

"You know," Grimaldi said, "I'm beginning to like your style."

Bolan was already several steps ahead of them.

11

De Keyserlei
Antwerp, Belgium

WHEN THEY WERE about fifteen yards from the entrance to the factory, Bolan felt something under the sole of his tactical boot. He held up his left fist to signal for Grimaldi and Lupin to stop and flipped down his night vision goggles. The scene was illuminated in fluorescent green. The Executioner glanced around and, seeing no one, scanned the ground immediately in front of him and lifted his foot. A partially crushed brass shell lay on the ground where he had stepped. A second shell casing was a few inches away. Both appeared to have come from a 9 mm pistol.

Grimaldi also flipped his goggles down and leaned back to whisper to Lupin, who had no night vision equipment.

The INTERPOL man nodded.

Bolan moved forward with renewed caution, his Beretta held at the combat-ready position, arms bent in front of his chest. This allowed for maximum speed of movement with the option of raising the weapon to fire in a millisecond. He advanced toward the door, the green tint providing an expansive and complete view of the area. Two erratic stains, most likely blood, spotted the area in front of the door. What appeared to be bloody partial footprints were present, as well.

Bolan stopped again and whispered to Grimaldi, "It looks like they dragged the bodies inside."

Grimaldi nodded and positioned himself off to the side of the door, aiming his SIG at the opening and gesturing for Lupin to step away from the line of fire. Bolan gripped the doorknob and twisted gingerly. It turned and he swung it open, stepping back to cover the opposite side of the interior. Seeing no assailants, Bolan shot forward, moving inside with a quick grace. The interior of the factory was dark, but his night vision goggles gave him a clear picture of everything.

The bodies of four men had been laid out just inside the door. Blood pooled in crescent halos around each of their heads.

The Executioner saw two more shell casings on the floor by the bodies. The aggressor must have shot the two men who were standing outside the door at a distance of approximately twenty-five yards—an impressive shot in the dark with a handgun. Both head shots, too. The killer had most likely been using a weapon with a sound suppressor so as not to alert the secondary guards inside. Those men had also been shot. It indicated more than one aggressor. Most likely they were dealing with at least two highly trained, well-equipped, professional killers—a killing team.

After stationing Lupin in wait by the door, Bolan and Grimaldi began a quick but systematic clearing of the building. Most of the interior walls had been knocked down, leaving expansive areas devoid of any furnishings. They followed a corridor down to a narrower hallway that offered a ninety-degree turn into a maze of thinly constructed walls. The steady hum of a generator was coming from one of the rooms. Bolan paused at the opening of the corridor and began slicing the pie as he edged around the corner. He could smell burning tobacco. Maybe these guys weren't so professional after all.

Bolan edged around the corner a bit more, giving him a partial view. A sliver of light outlined a door midway down the corridor. A pair of voices became audible. Bolan's glance at Grimaldi confirmed that he'd heard them, too.

The narrow corridor was a perfect ambush site...a kill zone. He and Grimaldi were wearing level 3, bullet-resistant vests under their BDUs, but that still left their extremities, not to mention their heads, vulnerable. The illuminated, closed door was approximately fifteen feet away, with about twenty feet of hallway on the opposite side. If the first distance could be covered fast enough, Bolan figured they'd have the element of surprise. The walls of the corridor appeared to be nothing more than cheap drywall, however, which would offer little in the way of ballistic cover.

Bolan started to edge back to confer with Grimaldi when the door opened, spilling a flash of light into the dark hallway and causing a flarelike explosion in the Executioner's night vision goggles. He flipped the goggles up on his forehead in time to see a man dressed in dark clothing raising a pistol, a long, Russian-style cigarette dangling from his lips.

The Executioner fired first, sending three rounds toward his adversary. The barrel of the other man's gun exploded in a burst of flame and Bolan felt a round zing by him on the left.

He fired again, and the gunman crumpled forward. A hand holding a pistol curled around the edge of the doorjamb, and the weapon spat several times.

Bolan had already moved out of the opening. Grimaldi fired his SIG in the direction of their new adversary as Lupin came running up.

"What's happening?" he asked.

Bolan pushed him back, out of their adversary's field of fire.

More rounds zipped by. Lupin crouched in response.

"Bad guy at nine o'clock," Grimaldi said, firing off another round. "He's in that room halfway down the hallway."

"The other units are almost here," Lupin said.

Bolan clamped his Beretta under his left arm, reached into the pocket of his BDU shirt and took out a stun grenade. Lupin's eyes widened as Bolan bent back the flanges of the pin and looked at Grimaldi.

"Give me a diversion," he said.

Grimaldi nodded and kicked the toe of his boot into the soft drywall, causing a large chunk to break away. He reached down and grabbed the broken piece. Switching his SIG to his left hand, Grimaldi leaned forward and threw the broken piece of drywall down the corridor. It smacked into the wall next to the doorway. Bolan released the safety flange on the flash-bang and began his count: one, two, three… He rolled the grenade down the corridor.

The hand curled around the door again, but the flash-bang, rolling like a discarded soft drink can, exploded just as it reached the open door.

The gun fell forward, out of their adversary's hand, and the man's body came after it. Bolan ran down the corridor, his Beretta at combat ready. He paused momentarily to kick the fallen weapon out of reach and then took a quick look into the room. Six bodies lay in a row on the floor next to a table, upon which sat some odds and ends: three wrist watches, several wallets, some currency and a business card.

Bolan continued inside and verified that each supine man was deceased. One of them, a large black man, whom Bolan assumed was Lumumba, appeared to have been shot through the mouth. Another's head had been twisted completely around so that his face was against the floor although his body lay on its back. The others all appeared to have suffered gunshots to the head and other parts of their bodies.

Grimaldi dragged in the guy from the hallway. He forced the still semi-dazed man onto the hard floor and quickly searched him. He found a knife in the man's pocket and two spare magazines for a Russian Tokarev pistol.

"Nine millimeter," Grimaldi said, holding up the mag. "Who you working for?"

The man said nothing.

Lupin addressed him in Russian. The man's eyes flickered slightly, but he still remained silent.

"We can interrogate him later," Bolan said. "We need to clear the rest of this floor. The backups can do upstairs."

Grimaldi nodded and gave the adversary's head a nudge with the SIG. "Don't go away. We'll be right back."

"Keep watch on him," Bolan said to Lupin. Although the Executioner appreciated Lupin's eagerness to accompany them, his lack of equipment and tactical expertise made him more of a liability. "We'll be right back."

The INTERPOL man nodded and held his small Walther PPK 6 in front of the prone man's face. He said something else in Russian, then looked at Bolan. "I do not know if he understands me, but I told him if he moved, I would kill him."

"Somehow I think he got the message," Grimaldi said with a grin.

Bolan was already at the door, checking the remainder of the hallway. He told Grimaldi to provide cover and went down the hall at a rapid pace. When he got to the end, he flipped down his night vision goggles and surveyed the interior. That last section of drywall had been an anomaly.

The rest of the place was wide open, containing a skeleton of wooden frames with no walls. Moving to the rear door, Bolan paused and checked it, noting the torn cobwebs. The latch had been pulled back to the unlocked position. Once Grimaldi was next to him, Bolan shoved open the door and did another quick peek. The door opened into an alleyway.

A big rat scurried across the ground to the apparent safety of some garbage cans. Nothing else moved.

Bolan heard the crack of two gunshots coming from the area they'd just left.

It had to involve Lupin.

Slamming the door and shoving the latch in place, Bolan and Grimaldi ran back down the corridor, stopping outside the room. Bolan, who'd gotten there first, edged around the door and saw Lupin, his head canted to the side, standing over the body of their last adversary. Two small, round holes were in the center of the man's forehead and twin ribbons of blood ran from both the holes and the man's mouth onto the cold concrete floor. A wisp of smoke lingered around the barrel of the Walther. Lupin turned to look at Bolan.

"He tried to make a break for it," Lupin said. "I guess he did not believe I would kill him."

The loss of possible intel bothered Bolan, but he didn't say anything. This whole mission had been plagued with bad luck from the beginning. He lowered his Beretta. In the distance he could hear the uneven wail of European police sirens.

The Van de Roovaart Hotel

STIEGLITZ TOOK A deep breath as he punched in the number on the special mobile phone. The call was answered on the first ring.

"What have you got to report?" the voice on the phone said.

He hadn't expected such a quick interrogative. Stieglitz started to take another breath when the voice spoke again, this time with a harsher edge. "I am waiting."

"Yes, sir," Stieglitz said, his nervousness raising the pitch of his voice. "I was merely calling to advise you that everything went as planned. We eliminated Grodovich's former partner, and Rovalev placed the stone on the body of the African."

A few seconds of silence were followed by a slightly more relaxed tone. "That is good. Where is the large stone now?"

"They are taking it to some man in the Diamond Quarter for appraisement and preparation."

"Has Rovalev been fully briefed on how I wish that to proceed?"

"Yes, sir."

"And the Americans?"

"I am awaiting a further report on them." Stieglitz glanced at his watch. "My latest information said they discovered the bodies in the meeting place and were working with the local police."

"What have they reported to their authorities regarding the diamond?"

Stieglitz held his breath. It was a question to which he had no answer. Trying to swallow, but finding his mouth dry, he managed to say, "I believe they are operating under the assumption that the African was here with a large quantity of conflict diamonds."

The voice became tense again. "I asked you what they have reported to their superiors."

Stieglitz hesitated, not knowing how to reply.

"You do not know," the voice asked. "Is that it?"

"I—I…" Stieglitz stammered.

"Find out." The tones were clipped, angry again. "Make certain the trail is obvious enough for them to follow. Is that clear?"

"Yes, sir. Of course, sir."

"Good. And remember our time constraints. Call me back with an update."

Stieglitz replied in the affirmative and listened for further instructions. He heard nothing. Waiting what he felt was an appropriate amount of time, he tentatively asked, "Is there anything else, sir?"

No response.

Stieglitz glanced at the screen to confirm the call had been terminated and then slipped the mobile back into his pocket.

Abandoned Factory
De Keyserlei Avenue

BOLAN WATCHED AS the police evidence technicians busied themselves photographing and collecting the array of shell casings from the floor of the old factory. He glanced at his watch. They'd been tied up here for the better part of an hour while Lupin explained to the Belgian authorities about the dead bodies and the events that had led to the firefight.

Grimaldi took a sip from his paper cup and nodded. "At least Lupin got us some decent hot chocolate. I'm kind of developing a taste for this stuff."

Bolan hadn't touched his. He knew that with each tick of the clock their main quarry, Grodovich, was getting farther and farther away.

"You going to drink yours?" Grimaldi asked.

The Executioner shook his head and motioned for Lupin to come over.

The INTERPOL man walked with slow deliberation, stopping in front of both of them. His face had a drawn, dour look.

"You wish to speak with me, Coop?" he said.

Bolan nodded. "How much longer are we going to be tied up here?"

Lupin shrugged. "As I told you, the police do not often see a homicide like this." The corners of his mouth tugged into a half smile and he looked at Grimaldi. "It's like something out of one of your American movies."

"That's right, pilgrim," Grimaldi said, doing an exaggerated imitation of John Wayne. "And make sure you remind them we're not giving up our guns."

Lupin laughed. "That is very good. His movies were popular when I was growing up." He stopped and snapped his fingers. "And what was it they called him?"

"The Duke," Grimaldi said.

"Of course." Lupin nodded. "American royalty. From now on, that is what I shall call you. No more Jacques."

Grimaldi grinned.

"We need to pick up Grodovich," Bolan said. "Find out about his involvement in all this."

Lupin turned serious again. "I have already done that. A BOLO, as you Americans say, has been issued. As soon as he is located, we will be notified. In the meantime, I must attend to matters here. The two dead officers were Belgians, so emotions are at a high level." He paused. "I feel a certain responsibility for their deaths."

"We hear you," Grimaldi said. "We lost one of ours a few days ago."

"In the meantime," Lupin said, his face regaining its merriment, "do you wish for more hot chocolates? I can send someone."

Bolan shook his head, silently assessing the situation.

Perhaps it would be better to wait until the Belgian authorities located Grodovich. It was their country, their city, and they certainly had more resources at their disposal.

"Very well, then," Lupin said. "The chief investigator will be here shortly to take your statements. I will translate."

With that, the INTERPOL man walked away.

The Diamond Quarter

GRODOVICH WATCHED AS Malachi Bloom cleaned off the stained surface of the large diamond with a camel-hair cloth. Mikhal stood beside them, looking around at the man's office. The giant seemed fascinated by the tools and machines. Rovalev stood on the other side of Bloom, never letting the gem out of his sight. Grodovich had assured both him and Stieglitz of Bloom's skill as a gemologist.

"Both Yuri and I have worked with him in the past," Grodovich had said. "And his work is second to none."

"Tell that to your friend Yuri when you see him again," Rovalev said.

That remark had begun to bother Grodovich a bit more than when the Black Wolf had originally said it.

Bloom stopped polishing and raised the stone to his mouth, exhaling a long breath onto its surface and then watching the fog evaporate. His shaggy eyebrows lifted and he muttered to himself as he began searching his desktop for something. Finally, among a sea of paperwork, he picked up a jeweler's loupe. Placing it on his glasses frame, he flipped the loupe down and scrutinized the large stone once again. After a few moments, he picked up a small, portable diamond detector and held the metal end against the stone. The green light shot across the gauge seconds later. Bloom's lower lip protruded and he set the detector down, nodded and murmured to himself.

"Never have I seen a stone this large or this flawless," he said in English, the only language he and Grodovich shared. "It rivals the Congolese Giant that was found in 1907."

"What's your estimate of its worth?" Grodovich asked.

"I need to do a closer examination," Bloom said. "Run some more tests, look for and mark the inclusions." He rolled his shoulders in a shrug.

"How long will that take?" Rovalev asked.

Bloom looked to the other man and shrugged again. "It can't be rushed. With something this large, each inclusion, or flaw, must be carefully sought out and marked so I know where the cuts are to be made."

"We don't want all that," Rovalev said. "We just need you to give us an estimate of its worth and prepare a parcel."

Bloom considered this. "Do you have the proper documentation as to where this stone was found?"

"We will need your expert help on that, as well," Grodovich said. "Papers verifying the Kimberley Process."

Bloom smiled, keeping his lips pressed together. "Such documentation takes a long time to prepare," he said. "As does the examination, cutting and polishing. If you want several good diamonds with fifty-eight facets each from this colossus, I will need at least a week."

"A week?" Grodovich smiled. He'd been expecting a tug-of-war with this wily bastard. It was Bloom's way of driving up the price of his services.

"We don't have that kind of time, old man," Rovalev said. "Prepare a parcel with the appropriate details and the Kimberley verification papers. And do it quickly."

Bloom's mouth twisted downward. "Alexander, your friend's impertinence is not appreciated."

"Listen," the Black Wolf said, "the World Diamond Council conference begins next week in New York and we intend to auction off the stone at that event."

Bloom's eyes widened as he looked up at Grodovich, who nodded.

The man considered this and raised an eyebrow. "You plan to auction this stone at the conference?" He blew out a derisive breath. "Leave it in my hands and I will get you a much better price."

"I already told you what we want," Rovalev said. "Now do it."

Bloom took a deep breath, looking back to the stone in his hand, his head bobbling like a buoy in choppy water. "It is impossible that I could do an adequate job in such a short time. You should have brought this to me earlier. Much earlier." He glanced at a calendar on the wall, seemed to do some mental calculations and then shook his head again. "No, it is not possible. I need to run some additional tests."

"What kind of tests?" Grodovich said.

Bloom flipped down the loupe again. "I'll need to determine the specific density, the amount of nitrogen infusion…" He paused and stared at the diamond through the magnifier again. "This stone is almost too perfect. Perhaps I should check something else now."

"Check what?" Grodovich asked.

Bloom didn't answer. Instead, he got up and went to a filing cabinet next to his desk. He opened the drawer and withdrew a long, iridescent tube attached to a plastic handle.

"Light rays," Bloom said. "They register at certain frequencies—" He stopped suddenly and gasped.

Grodovich followed the old man's gaze and saw that

Rovalev had his Tokarev pistol out and was pointing it directly at Bloom.

"What are you doing?" Grodovich asked.

Mikhal lumbered over and stood beside Grodovich, who placed a calming palm on the giant's chest. He did not want Rovalev to shoot his protector.

Rovalev told everyone to be quiet as he removed his mobile phone and pressed some buttons. Presently, he was speaking in Russian to someone, Stieglitz, most probably, and listening intently.

From what Grodovich could discern from the one-sided conversation, Rovalev had told Stieglitz about the delay and Bloom's desire to do additional tests.

Rovalev listened, ended the call and placed the mobile back into his pocket. Keeping the pistol extended, Rovalev walked over and took the device from Bloom's hands. He set it on top of the filing cabinet and then gave Bloom a backhanded slap. The man's head jerked and a look of terror filled his eyes.

Rovalev glanced toward Grodovich and Mikhal. "Go back to the hotel and pack. We will be leaving Belgium shortly."

Grodovich didn't like the sound of that but knew he couldn't argue. Obviously, Stieglitz had given Rovalev specific instructions. He nodded for Mikhal to head toward the door.

"Alexander, where are you going?" Bloom said, his voice brittle with terror. "What did this man say to you?'

Oh, that's right, Grodovich thought. The old man did not understand Russian. He paused and tried to make his smile as reassuring as possible.

"Do not worry, Malachi," he said. "My impetuous associate has a specific set of instructions for you. I suggest you follow them with the utmost care."

He turned and left, listening as Rovalev began speaking in slow, deliberate English.

"Listen to me, you bastard. This is what you are going to do…"

Grodovich felt a twinge of pity for the old man. He had always appreciated Bloom's artistry.

The Diamantwijk District Police Station

IT WAS ZERO-SEVEN-THIRTY by the time they finished giving their statements. As they stood in the hallway outside the row of offices, Lupin spoke to the chief inspector in Flemish. They shook hands and Lupin turned back to Bolan.

"The inspector is satisfied with the accounting of the incident," Lupin said. "He also wishes me to thank you for your assistance."

Bolan looked at the man and nodded.

Lupin continued. "He must go to see the families of the two officers who were killed." He paused and looked away a moment. "A difficult task, to say the least, but it will give their families some small solace to know that the men we believe responsible were also killed."

"If they were the only shooters," Bolan said. "The ballistics might be able to tell you that, if you recover any projectiles."

Lupin nodded. He flashed a weary smile. "Well, since I have kept you up all night, may I take you both to a fabulous restaurant not too far from here, where we can get the most *magnifique*—"

"Have they picked up Grodovich yet?' Bolan asked.

Lupin canted his head slightly as one side of his mouth tugged downward. "Alas, no. Not as of yet. But, as I said, the BOLO—"

"When we entered that room I saw several items on

the table," Bolan said. "Two wallets, three wrist watches, some currency and a business card."

Lupin raised his eyebrows. "You must have a photographic memory. I cannot recall any of that."

"The bodies were placed in a neat row, which seems odd," Bolan said. "And why would that stuff be on the table?"

Lupin's brow furrowed. "An excellent question." He turned to the inspector and they conversed in Flemish. The inspector went to a nearby desk and picked up a phone. After dialing and giving some instructions, he turned back and said something else to Lupin.

"They are bringing the items to us now," Lupin said.

Approximately ten minutes later a uniformed policewoman walked in with seven clear plastic bags. Each bag had been sealed with red evidence tape and a white inventory sheet was paper clipped to each one. The woman laid the items on the desk.

Bolan sorted through the plastic bags, though he couldn't read the lists describing what the wallets contained, because they were in Dutch. He picked up the one with the business card. One side was in Hebrew, the other in English.

Malachi Bloom
Gemologist

An address and phone number were printed underneath.

Bolan wondered why Bloom's card was sitting on that table in front of four dead men, but something else was bothering him, too.

Grodovich... Diamonds... Hot rocks... Rad—

Somehow, it was all coming back to diamonds.

12

The Diamond Quarter

Malachi Bloom's shop looked like it had been there forever. The windows were filthy, which might be one of the reasons no one had paid undue notice to what had occurred inside the shop. Bolan and Grimaldi stood near the door as more police and crime scene technicians shuffled through. Lupin had attempted several phone calls to the shop on their way there but had received no answer.

"It is still relatively early," he said with a weary smile. "Perhaps he is a late riser.

When they'd arrived, Lupin tried the door and found it open. They entered and saw a man leaning forward in front of a closet door, a belt looped around his neck. His face was a dark purplish-red, his teeth set in a distended tongue.

Lupin had rushed forward and started fumbling with the belt, saying, "He may still be alive."

Bolan unclipped his Espada knife and flipped it open. He stepped over and severed the belt with one smooth stroke.

The old man's body slumped against Lupin, who lowered the limp form to the floor. Bolan could tell the man was dead, but he let the INTERPOL agent check him anyway.

Lupin heaved a sigh, stood up and said, "I must summon the authorities."

Several hours later, Bolan glanced at his watch and estimated that it was close to midnight at Stony Man Farm. He took out his satellite phone and told Grimaldi he was going to call Hal.

Grimaldi's face looked strained as he nodded. "I hope you wake him up."

"Not much chance of that," Bolan said. "I have it on good authority that he hardly ever sleeps when we're on a mission."

Grimaldi snorted. "Oh yeah, I guess it was just wishful thinking on my part. Misery loves company."

Bolan wouldn't have minded taking a combat nap, either. They hadn't slept in more than thirty hours, but he'd wait until the mission was complete. He stepped out into the late morning sunshine and dialed the number. Brognola answered with a gruff "Hello" after the fourth ring.

Bolan gave him a quick rundown, ending with, "We still haven't been able to run our buddy Grodovich to the ground. The Belgian authorities have a BOLO out on him."

"Oh yeah?" Brognola snorted. "Well, they should've looked harder. I just saw an interview with him on the news. He was at some airport in Belgium announcing his travel plans."

"The airport?"

"Yep. Aaron is still verifying it, but it appears he's on his way to Venezuela via a chartered flight."

"Venezuela?" Bolan said. The news stunned him. "The man's wanted for questioning in two separate homicide investigations. How could they let him slip out of the country?"

"Two homicide investigations?" Brognola asked. "I thought you said the gemologist hung himself?"

"That's the way it was set up," Bolan said. "There was an unsigned suicide note on the old guy's computer, but he also had what appeared to be a scrape on the left side of his head. Like somebody slammed him against a wall or something."

Brognola grunted.

"So," Bolan said, "you say Grodovich was on the news?"

"Yeah, I'll have Aaron send you the clip. Basically he said he was leaving to confer with some business associates in Venezuela and then he planned on attending the World Diamond Council Conference in New York next week. He was spouting off some bullshit about having an announcement of such magnitude that it will shock the world." Brognola laughed. "Yeah, right."

Diamonds again, Bolan thought.

"Anyway," Brognola said, "if he is mixed up with conflict diamonds, the Venezuela trip makes sense. It's one of the few countries that refuses to abide by the Kímberley Process."

Bolan had already thought of that. "And they always have a contingent of dealers at the World Diamond Council conference auction."

"True. You want Aaron to book you and Jack on a flight to Caracas, or do you want to wait till our boy arrives in the Big Apple?" Brognola cleared his throat. "I don't need to remind you that Venezuela isn't exactly friendly territory these days."

Bolan remained silent, going over his options. He watched as a group of Hasidic Jews, dressed in their black outfits and hats, mingled with a growing crowd on the other side of the street, conversing and pointing toward the shop and police cars.

Malachi Bloom must have been a popular man, Bolan thought.

"Striker, you still there?" Brognola asked.

"I am," Bolan said. "I'll get back to you about our travel plans."

He terminated the call and stepped back into the shop. Lupin stood conferring with another detective in plain clothes. Grimaldi yawned and blinked several times.

"Man, I need some shut-eye," he said. "Bad."

"Relax," Bolan replied. "Pretty soon you'll have all the rest you need."

"Oh?"

Bolan nodded. "It's going to be a long flight to Venezuela."

Somewhere over the Atlantic Ocean

As soon as Stieglitz was certain both Grodovich and his giant friend were asleep, he motioned for Rovalev to join him in the Learjet's small conference room. The Black Wolf rose from his seat and moved down the aisle, stooping slightly because of the low ceiling.

Stieglitz closed the door behind them and sat in one of the two chairs. He waved for Rovalev to take the other.

"It is regrettable that your men were killed," Stieglitz said. "But apparently, the business card, which they were supposed to plant on the African's body, was discovered in good time."

Rovalev shrugged. "They were mercenaries, paid to do a job. Such men know the risks."

"We shall have more of them at your disposal when we get to New York." Stieglitz leaned forward and spoke softly. "You are certain no one followed you after you delivered the stone to the embassy?"

"Of course," Rovalev said. His manner was confident, assured.

"And at the old man's shop," Stieglitz said. "You left the trail of clues, as I directed?"

Rovalev stared at him with those feral eyes. Stieglitz felt a shiver go down his spine and knew that Rovalev could easily kill him before he got out of the room. The man was brutally efficient, and from what Stieglitz had seen thus far, he had no compunction about killing. But this Black Wolf was also a professional and obviously committed to completing the task at hand.

Stieglitz felt some small measure of comfort that he'd been able to read Rovalev so easily.

"They will find the aborted versions of the Kimberley Process papers," Rovalev said. "And thanks to our press conference at the airport, the Americans are probably already chartering their plane."

Stieglitz was certain, as well, that the Americans would have reported these latest developments to their superiors in the US intelligence community. The large stone and the Semtex explosive compound would be delivered to the Russian Embassy in New York by diplomatic pouch while they dazzled the Venezuelans with the array of stones they'd taken from the African. The Venezuelans would be more than happy to act as surrogate partners to provide Grodovich with entry into the diamond auction once again… Then things would end with a bang instead of a whimper.

"The two Americans are now expendable," Stieglitz said. "They will be taken care of when they arrive in Venezuela."

Rovalev nodded. "I shall look forward to that task."

"No, I have arranged for others to do that. You have a more important role."

The other man's head lowered slightly, his gaze penetrating.

It was time to brief Rovalev about the remainder of the plan. Or at least almost all of the remainder. Stieglitz leaned forward again and spoke in a voice hardly above a whisper.

"As I told you in Antwerp, the large stone is a synthetic, which was the reason we could not allow Bloom to perform any further tests. He was suspicious only because of his vast expertise with gems. We anticipated that possibility."

"Can a layman tell the difference?" Rovalev asked.

Stieglitz shook his head. "Only an expert gemologist using ultraviolet lighting. It is a real diamond, only man-made. But to all the world, it must appear to be a conflict diamond. That is imperative."

"Understood," Rovalev said.

"Its only purpose is to assure a full attendance at the World Diamond Council auction," Stieglitz said. "To pique the world's curiosity and allow Grodovich to enter the auction site."

Rovalev continued to watch him.

"Once we arrive in New York," Stieglitz continued, "you will have additional assistance. The final phase of the operation is crucial."

"And you are going to reveal this final phase to me now?"

Stieglitz still felt the urge to move cautiously. If he told Rovalev every aspect of what was to come, the man might lose his nerve.

But no, he thought. He has no money and no resources, either in Venezuela or the United States. And he would be a marked man by the Kremlin if he did not follow through. They were both on a one-way track. It was full speed toward success…or death.

He got up and went to the cabin door, opened it a crack and verified that Grodovich and the giant were still asleep.

He returned to his seat and looked across the table at Rovalev.

"When Grodovich is at the auction," Stieglitz said, "dazzling everyone with the size and prospective value of the large stone, we will set off twin explosions, killing everyone inside."

Rovalev's right eyebrow twitched slightly. "Including Grodovich?"

Stieglitz nodded. "He is not to be made aware of that, of course."

Rovalev gave a slight nod, his expression placid.

Stieglitz was certain that the vaunted Black Wolf had not expected this new information.

But should he be told the rest of it? The most crucial part?

"The explosives are being delivered to our embassy in New York," Stieglitz continued. "Our experts there are fashioning two suitcase bombs to be detonated by a device broadcasting a low-frequency radio signal, which you will have. You will program it on another floor. A timer will allow you to be safely out of the building when the bombs go off."

Rovalev said nothing. For the first time Stieglitz caught a look of trepidation in the man's tawny eyes.

"The explosion will be linked to local Chechen gangsters. A recording claiming responsibility, in retaliation for Grodovich killing his Chechen partner, has already been prepared. It will absolve us of any responsibility."

Rovalev squinted as he stroked his beard.

"What is it?" Stieglitz asked. "What is wrong?"

"What is the purpose of all this? It seems pointless to blow everything up to conceal the fact that your large diamond is a fake."

Stieglitz twisted his mouth into a frown. He hadn't

wanted to divulge the entirety of the plan until the eleventh hour, but Rovalev's doubts left him little choice.

"This auction is a yearly international event," Stieglitz said. "Virtually ninety percent of the world's newest gems will be in that room at the same time."

Rovalev laughed. "Are you planning on using a rake to go through the debris?"

"There will be no recoveries," Stieglitz said, his voice harsh. He took a second to compose himself and began whispering again. "The suitcases will contain cesium. Once the radioactivity has spread throughout the room, the diamonds and everything else will be unrecoverable."

Rovalev considered this for a moment. His lips twitched into a smile. "So the diamonds that the Kremlin has in its private stockpile, even the synthetic ones, will increase in value."

"Exponentially so," Stieglitz said. "It will allow us to take control of the world diamond market and reestablish our economy, despite the ongoing sanctions by the West."

"A bold move," Rovalev said. "Both daring and cunning. As the Americans say, a diamond is forever."

"Unless," Stieglitz said, "it is radioactive."

13

Berchem Airport
Antwerp, Belgium

BOLAN, Grimaldi and Lupin were the only passengers on
the plane. While Aaron had been setting up the chartered
flight, Lupin had used his INTERPOL connections to get
their weapons and equipment rushed through the airport so
they could pursue Grodovich to Venezuela. Grimaldi, who
was clearly exhausted, had grumbled a bit as the pilot took
off, saying the guy flew like an amateur, but he'd dropped
off to sleep soon after they'd achieved cruising altitude.
Lupin had grabbed a pillow as soon as they'd boarded and
told them to wake him when they got to Caracas.

Bolan tried to sleep as well but found it difficult. The
words of the dying traitor, Lawrence Burns, kept echoing
in Bolan's mind: *"Listen, Grodovich... Diamonds... Hot
rocks... Rad—"*

What had Burns been trying to tell him? Was it a message or simply the mixed-up ranting of a man on the edge
of mortality?

Which brought Bolan back to Alexander Grodovich.
He'd apparently engineered the killing of a lot of people
in Antwerp, including his former partner, to get hold of

some conflict diamonds. He was on his way to the annual World Diamond Council conference in New York. But how was all that related to Burns and his Russian partner? It seemed like a lot of trouble just to get a conflict diamond into the auction.

Burns had said he and Kropotkan had something to trade. Something so significant the US government would overlook his defecting to Russia. And it had to be something the Russians were set on keeping under wraps. Conflict diamonds… "Hot rocks"? And what about "rad"? Bolan shook his head.

A riddle wrapped in a mystery inside an enigma…

Bolan glanced across the aisle at Lupin, who slumbered soundly, occasionally saying something in what sounded like French or Russian.

The INTERPOL agent had promised to ask his superiors to push through a court order in Belgium commanding that Grodovich be brought in for questioning.

It's too bad we couldn't tie him to the murders in Moscow, too, Bolan thought. He glanced at his watch and estimated they still had a good three to four hours of flying time left. Bolan reclined his seat and placed his head against the pillow.

It was time to take another shot at an extended combat nap.

Caracas, Venezuela

GRODOVICH SAT BESIDE Pedro Alberto Martinez on the sidewalk veranda, enjoying the shade cast by their table's umbrella. Beyond the open foyer of decorative green stones and marble stairs, cars whizzed by on the busy street. Stieglitz sat across from them, his back to the street, apparently basking in the security that Rovalev, who was seated at an adjacent table with Mikhal, provided. The fresh spring air was laden with the scent of nearby bougainvillea blossoms.

Martinez smiled and shook his head. "Where did you find that Russian giant?" He spoke in heavily accented English, the only language the three of them shared. "He is like *grand toro*. I would imagine, from the looks of him, he is quite the ideal bodyguard."

"Let us just say," Grodovich said, smiling as he sipped from his glass of lemonade, "that he has proven himself many times."

Martinez grinned also and nodded. "It is good to have such a man by your side in times like these. And his amigo, the bearded one. He is very dangerous, too, no?"

"Yes," Grodovich said. "But they are not friends, only business associates."

Martinez laughed and clapped his hands together. "Do you wish to order now?" He motioned and a pretty girl wearing a tight red blouse and skirt strolled over to them. She parted her lips in a demure smile and spoke to Martinez in Spanish. He began to give her explicit instructions and then paused. "I assume you all wish to sample our magnificent *bistec*, er, steak. I am correct?"

Grodovich looked at Stieglitz, who nodded. The man had not said more than a handful of words since they'd sat down, but his piercing gaze reminded Grodovich this was still not his play. He was merely a pawn.

No, he thought, better that I fashion myself as a knight. The black knight.

It had always been his favorite chess piece. Although not as powerful as the bishop or the rook, the knight made up for it with mobility.

"And *el grande*," Martinez said, pointing at Mikhal. "Does the giant eat his meat raw?"

Grodovich glanced at Mikhal, who, from his expression, knew he was being talked about. Grodovich repeated Martinez's question in Russian.

"Nyet," Mikhal said, adding that he was a man, not a beast.

Grodovich relayed the message to Martinez, whose eyebrows rose like twin caterpillars.

"Por favor, tell him I was only joking." Martinez smiled nervously. "I am sorry to have offended him. I meant it only as a compliment."

Grodovich translated. Mikhal stared at Martinez for a few moments, then snorted as he nodded his head.

The waitress had begun to appear nervous. She asked if they needed anything else.

"Only to be left alone until our meal is ready," Grodovich said in Spanish.

The girl's eyes widened and she was gone in a flash.

"Ah, *su espanol es muy perfecto*," Martinez said. "It is too bad Señor Stieglitz does not understand it."

"Perhaps it is time we get down to business," Grodovich said. He reached inside his jacket pocket and withdrew a small envelope. It contained half a dozen stones that they'd taken from Lumumba. He glanced at Stieglitz, who nodded. Grodovich handed the envelope to Martinez, who wiped his palms on his trouser legs before accepting it.

Grodovich watched the Venezuelan dump the stones into his palm. With his other hand Martinez reached into his pocket, took out a jeweler's loupe and checked the stones, one by one. Afterward, he carefully replaced them in the envelope and handed them back to Grodovich.

"An interesting selection," Martinez said, his friendly expression giving way to one of absolute neutrality. "High-quality gems, of course, but after your most recent announcement, I was expecting something a bit more, how shall I say it, spectacular?"

Grodovich shrugged. "This was but a small sample."

Martinez nodded. "And what about *el grande*? The stone you said rivaled the Congolese Giant?"

"That one is being kept in a safe place," Grodovich said. "For the moment." He replaced the envelope into his pocket and withdrew a second piece of paper. "Here is a copy of the packet that was prepared in Antwerp. It has all the specifics of the gem, including the carets listing. It is still rough, but as you can see, it not only rivals the Congolese Giant in size but surpasses it."

Martinez took out a pair of glasses and scanned the document, his mustache twitching as he read. "This is very interesting."

"Unfortunately," Grodovich said, "we recovered the gem but not the certification papers. Thus, we need your assistance, the assistance of your established diamond trading company, in introducing the stone at the World Diamond Council auction on Monday."

Martinez smirked. "Of course. This will not be a problem…" He paused and lifted an eyebrow. "What percentage of the sale would I be afforded for my help, or rather the help of my company?"

Grodovich smiled back. He knew it would come down to this final, essential banter. It was the part of the game he knew best: the ebb and flow of negotiations. But this time, Stieglitz had informed him he was not to barter. "Give the foreigner whatever he wants to assure our entry into the auction room," Stieglitz had said. "Do you understand?"

"What did you have in mind?" Grodovich asked.

Martinez pursed his lips, as if he were really contemplating it. Grodovich knew the man would jump at anything above the standard fifteen percent. "I am hesitant to speculate…without the courtesy of examining the merchandise…"

Stieglitz tapped his knuckles on the tabletop. His glare was the picture of impatience. No wonder the man had never sought entry into Russia's burgeoning business opportunities. He'd been born to assume the role of the typical, unimaginative government bureaucrat.

"We are prepared to offer you the standard fifteen percent," Grodovich said.

Martinez blew out a slow breath. Grodovich knew the Venezuelan had sensed the urgency in Stieglitz. He started to speak, but Grodovich cut him off.

"Since I am certain of the immensity of the price, we shall offer you twenty percent." He glanced at Stieglitz, who nodded fractionally. "But this is our final offer."

Martinez's lips twitched again, the involuntary tic that had always allowed Grodovich to manipulate the Venezuelan. But Stieglitz was the ultimate authority in this deal, and if his bosses back at the Kremlin were upset at this offer, so be it.

"That is very generous," Martinez said. "I am stunned."

"No problema," Grodovich said. *"El gusto es mio."*

Martinez laughed and picked up his wineglass. "Okay, it is a deal." He clicked his glass against Grodovich's. "Drink up, and I shall order more wine for all of us. And after our feast, we shall all go to my private resort on *las islas de Las Roques*." He turned toward Stieglitz. "You have never seen such a beautiful place." Turning back to Grodovich, Martinez said, "It has been a long time since you visited, but tell them, is it not beautiful and serene?"

"With the most beautiful women in the world to care for your every whim,' Grodovich answered.

Martinez laughed loudly. "I will make sure we have plenty of women on hand."

Grodovich laughed, too, but caught the eye of Stieglitz. The man was biting his upper lip, as if contemplating something other than the prospects of pleasure.

Caracas, Venezuela

AFTER HE FINISHED checking his equipment, Bolan stepped onto the hotel balcony and called Stony Man Farm. Brognola answered with his usual alacrity.

"Caracas, huh? Well, lots of pretty girls, and at least we're in the same time zone now, more or less," he said. "That's a plus, right?"

"That remains to be seen," Bolan said. "It depends on how much red tape we'll have to cut through."

Brognola sighed. "Yeah, I know it's probably a bit cumbersome at times, having François going through official channels."

"That's an understatement."

"Where's he now?" Brognola asked.

"He went to check in with the local authorities and his superiors at INTERPOL headquarters. Asked Jack and me to stay here. It seems Americans are still *persona non grata* down here."

"Can't you say you're Canadians?"

"Jack's a bit too brash to make that believable."

"I'm starting to regret hooking you guys up with INTERPOL," Brognola said. "You'd have been better off handling things the old-fashioned way."

"My sentiments exactly," Bolan said.

Grimaldi pushed his head outside and said, "He's baaack."

"Hal, Lupin's back," Bolan said. "I have to go."

"Okay. Watch yourselves."

Bolan ended the call and stepped back inside. Lupin

stood by the desk with a wine bottle in an ice bucket. He held up the bottle and tilted his head in an inquisitive way.

"My French blood craves wine every afternoon. Would you care to join me?"

Bolan shook his head. Grimaldi glanced at Bolan and then also gave his head a shake.

"What did you find out?" Bolan asked.

"I have, as you Americans say, the good news and the bad news." Lupin was inserting the corkscrew. After a few deft twists, he pulled the cork free with a pop. He picked up a glass from the dresser and poured some wine from the bottle. "Which one do you wish to hear first?"

"Give us the good news," Grimaldi said. "I need a boost."

Lupin took a sip as he jerked with laughter. "I have to remember that one." He took another drink. "Okay, the local authorities have agreed to hold Monsieur Grodovich pending any extradition proceedings."

"Great," Grimaldi said. "Let's go pick him up and we can let the courts do their work." He clapped his hands together. "Lots of gorgeous women down this way. Did you know that Venezuela has won more Miss World contests than any other country?"

Lupin swallowed some more wine and nodded vigorously. "You are a man after my own heart. Are you part French?"

"What's the bad news?" Bolan asked.

Lupin took a deep breath and sighed. "Unfortunately, due to the privacy laws here, they require written consent for the government to locate individuals residing or visiting here."

"Sounds like they're going to be a lot of help," Grimaldi said.

Lupin laughed and drained his glass. "Are you sure you will not join me?"

"No, thanks," Bolan said. "And I think you'd better level it off so we can start beating the bushes for Grodovich."

Lupin held up his index finger and waggled it.

"Mon ami," he said, "this is not my first trip to Venezuela." He shot them an exaggerated wink and sipped more wine. "I have used my contacts here to locate our quarry. He is with Pedro Alberto Martinez, a local crime boss who masquerades as a businessman. He and Grodovich have a long history together."

"Where are they exactly?" Bolan asked.

"On an island off the coast. The *Los Roques* archipelago. The main island is a national park, but Martinez owns a resort on an adjacent island. He is entertaining Grodovich there."

"I've been to *Los Roques*," Bolan said. "It's about half an hour away by plane, and the flights are restricted."

"Ah, yes," Lupin said. "But if we rent our own airplane, perhaps we can find a capable pilot."

Grimaldi flashed a big grin.

"If it has wings or a rotor," he said, "I can fly it."

La Casa del Suenos
Las Islas de Los Roques

STIEGLITZ WALKED INSIDE the large, brightly lit room and saw Grodovich with his arm draped over the bare shoulders of a woman and a glass dangling from his other hand. They were both laughing as they watched the giant Mikhal holding up two nearly nude females, one in each hand.

The sight amused him. Neither of these men had much longer to live.

Rovalev was suddenly beside him. Stieglitz turned and scanned the man, checking to see if he had been imbibing. He had no glass.

"You are not partaking in the festivities?" Stieglitz asked.

Rovalev shook his head.

"Good," Stieglitz said. "We will be leaving shortly. They are preparing the boat and plane as we speak."

Rovalev nodded.

"The Americans are in Caracas," Stieglitz said. "They will be coming here soon."

"Do you wish me to prepare a reception party?" Rovalev asked.

Stieglitz shook his head. "They will be attended to by others. It has been arranged. As I said, we will be leaving very soon." He took one more look at the giant, who had lifted both women above his massive head. "We have a more pressing matter in New York."

14

Airstrip
Islas de Los Roques

BY THE TIME their rented plane touched down on the dusty airstrip of Los Islas de los Roques it was almost dark. The airstrip itself was gravel and dirt with occasional patches of asphalt. The ground crew had set up orange pylons that directed them toward an array of one-story buildings and a big welcome sign. To the west, the sun was a yellow globe descending into the ocean.

Bolan glanced at their pilot, who worked for the tour company—a development Grimaldi had not been happy with. He was standing by the plane smoking a cigarette.

"Where's the target?" Bolan asked, shifting the backpack that contained his weapons.

"The next island over," Lupin said, pointing east. "We will need to rent a boat to get there."

"And what assurance do we have that the plane will be waiting for us when we get back?" Bolan asked.

"*Mon ami,* I am wounded," Lupin said. He held up a key attached to a plastic tab. "He will not be able to start the plane without inserting this into the instrument panel."

"All right," Bolan said, looking around. A few men

were meandering about on the airstrip next to a series of hangers. A couple ramshackle buildings, restaurants set on pylons, hovered tenuously three feet above the water. A dim set of lights illuminated an almost empty dining area. "Let's get our boat."

The negotiation took a matter of minutes. Their guide looked to be in his mid-thirties in his dark sunglasses and bandanna tied over his head and Bolan listened as Lupin conversed with the man in Spanish. Although the Executioner also spoke the language, he didn't mention that to Lupin.

The guide led them to a pier where several boats of varying length were moored. He stopped in front of a white speedboat with a big outboard motor angled just out of the water.

Bolan did a quick assessment of the craft. It looked to be in pretty good shape, which meant they'd be able to traverse the distance rather quickly. The seating was limited, but it would hold the four of them easily. Adding Grodovich for the return trip would be a bit more cramped, but doable.

They got on board and the guide untied the bowline, hopped on the tail and pulled the cord of the outboard. The engine roared to life and the guide tilted it into the water, steering them deftly away from the pier. Ahead the view of the sun was almost halfway obscured by the dark water. Bolan took out his cell phone and did a quick directional reading, just in case they had to find their way back on their own. He replaced the phone in its waterproof container.

The Executioner couldn't shake a growing uneasiness about this mission. Although Lupin seemed capable, Bolan wondered just how reliable the INTERPOL man's information was and if he'd covered all the bases. So far, Grodovich had managed to stay a couple moves ahead at every turn. Would he really be so lax as to leave himself isolated and unprotected on a Caribbean island?

"Any idea how many men he's got with him?" Bolan asked.

Lupin shrugged. "My source told me that Martinez has his usual contingent of bodyguards. Perhaps five or six. And Grodovich has a giant accompanying him everywhere. You might have seen him on the television news."

Bolan had seen the guy, and he'd also gotten an update from Brognola that the man-mountain was named Mikhal Markovich, a Russian inmate who had been incarcerated in Krasnoyarsk and released with Grodovich.

"Regardless," Lupin said, "I have it on good authority that Martinez imported a group of prostitutes for his guests. It is my assumption that at some point in the evening, Monsieur Grodovich will be alone with one of these beautiful young ladies." He paused to flash a smile.

"Está ahí," the guide said.

Bolan could see a black shape rising out of the water ahead of them, but he didn't see any lights. He estimated that they'd traveled about a mile and a half from the other island. Certainly a challenging swim if they ended up without a boat.

When they were a hundred feet from shore Lupin told the man to cut the engine. He did and the boat silently continued toward the beach, propelled by the waves. When they got close enough to shore the guide hopped out and began pushing the boat with his hands. The water was at mid-thigh level. Lupin also jumped out and began helping him push, followed by Bolan and Grimaldi. When they reached ankle-depth water, they each grabbed the framework of the boat and carried it to shore.

The guide mumbled something and Lupin said, "He

says we'll have to put it a bit farther up. The tide's coming in."

After they'd stashed it just below some shrubbery, Bolan reached in and grabbed his backpack. He checked the night vision goggles and fastened them on his head and strapped on his pistol belt with the Beretta 93R in a tactical holster on the right side and an ammunition pouch with two extra magazines on the left. He brushed his right side pants pocket to verify that his Espada knife was still clipped in place and removed a tube of camo paint from his backpack.

"We'd better paint up if we're going to surprise him," he said.

"Do you mean camouflage?" Lupin asked, his brow wrinkling. "I would rather not."

Bolan finished smearing the black paint on his face and held it toward Lupin. "Want me to do it for you?"

The INTERPOL man sighed, took the tube and gingerly smeared a few lines on his forehead, cheeks and chin.

Bolan could tell this guy had little military experience. He took the tube and added a few more streaks that would help him blend in with the dark night. Grimaldi took the tube next.

"You'd better stay back with the boat," Bolan said.

Grimaldi frowned and nodded. "I was just thinking the same thing, just in case our buddy here gets cold feet and takes off without us."

Lupin clicked his tongue. "I should have thought of that."

"You made sure the pilot wouldn't leave without us," Bolan said. "How far is the resort?"

"Not even one kilometer."

"Let's get going then." Bolan walked toward the sand bar with Lupin behind him.

As they began scaling the ridge, Bolan heard Grimaldi

yell and then grunt. As he turned, he heard a Taser clicking and felt the jolt of needles piercing the back of his left thigh. A millisecond later his muscles stiffened and he hit the ground. The pain and paralysis continued as Lupin stooped over him and pulled the Beretta from its holster.

He stepped back and pointed Bolan's own weapon right at him.

"Regrettably, *mon ami*," the INTERPOL man said, "we are a bit too late to catch our quarry. And I have a few questions to ask of you and your partner."

Bolan said nothing, trying to work the residual pain out of his muscles.

No wonder Grodovich was always one step ahead of us, he thought. He had an inside man.

BOLAN AND GRIMALDI sat surrounded by five men, all of whom were armed. Lupin and the tour guide had been joined by three others, who moved out of the shadows of the beach. All three carried submachine guns. Lupin still had Bolan's Beretta and the tour guide had Grimaldi's SIG Sauer. Lupin spoke to them in Spanish, saying he had to get some information before killing them.

At least I know what his plan is, Bolan thought. He also had the Espada knife in his pocket. He hadn't made a show of checking it after they'd gotten out of the boat, so there was a chance Lupin hadn't seen it in the moonlight.

"How much are they paying you?" Bolan asked.

Lupin turned and smiled. "A lot, *mon ami*. Enough to allow an underpaid civil servant to indulge his epicurean tastes." The smile faded. "And now, I must ask you a few questions. Answer truthfully and I will leave you and your friend on this island. Once I am safely away, I will send someone to take you back to the mainland."

"You won't kill us, huh?" Grimaldi said.

Lupin shook his head. "Not if you give me the information I desire. You have my word." He rolled his shoulders slightly. "After all the time we spent together, I have acquired a certain fondness for you both." His right eyed closed in a wink.

"What do you want to know?" Bolan asked.

Lupin trained his gaze on him. "My employers wish to know what the American defector, Burns, and his Russian paramour told you in Moscow," he said. "They also wish to know exactly what you have reported to your superiors in the United States."

"Who's paying you?" Bolan asked.

Lupin shook his head, his expression still amicable. "I ask the questions. You answer them. Understood?"

"If it's the Russians," Bolan said, "we can double it."

Lupin laughed. "Now you sound like Sean Connery in that James Bond movie." He shook his head and the smile faded from his face once more. Lupin yelled in Spanish for the man standing behind Grimaldi to grab him.

The man shifted his machine gun around so the strap kept it suspended on his back and then grabbed Grimaldi's arms. Stepping forward, Lupin backhanded Grimaldi across the face.

"Is that all you got?" Grimaldi asked, a trickle of blood winding down from his lips.

"No," Lupin said. "I have much, much more." He repeated the slap and then danced away as the man struggled to hold Grimaldi. Lupin motioned for one of the other thugs to assist in the restraint. "Paco, take out your knife and get ready to cut that one's ear off." Lupin pointed to Grimaldi. "But not until I tell you."

The tour guide, who had been playing with the SIG Sauer, spinning it like a toy pistol, grinned. He stuck the pistol into the front of his pants and took a long knife with a wicked-looking blade from its sheath on his belt.

"You see, Cooper," Lupin said, "I am pressed for time. I am anxious to begin my early retirement, so I need your responses to be honest and forthcoming. I am certain that if I were to torture you, you would do your best to resist. But watching your friend and partner endure mutilation and pain will no doubt elicit the answers I seek in a more timely fashion."

Paco, the tour guide, grabbed Grimaldi's left ear, pulling it outward. The man's teeth gleamed white in the moonlight as he wiped the edge of the blade against Grimaldi's cheek.

"You're a chicken-shit son of a bitch, Lupin," Grimaldi said, gritting his teeth from the pain.

Bolan did a quick assessment: He probably wouldn't get a better chance. Two of the potential assailants were busy holding Grimaldi, and Paco seemed to be either stupid, unfamiliar with firearms or both. That left Lupin and the third guy with the machine gun, who looked fairly capable. He'd kept his weapon combat-ready since the little drama had begun. Bolan decided it would be safest to kill him first. He pretended to lose his balance and dug his fingers into the sand.

"Okay, okay," he said, starting to stand.

"I did not say you could move," Lupin shouted. "Sit—"

"Don't tell him shit!" Grimaldi yelled at the top of his voice. "I can take it!"

Lupin's gaze wavered for a few seconds, as did the third guy with the machine gun. Bolan brought his left hand upward and flung sand into the man's eyes. As Bolan had anticipated, the guy pulled the trigger, but the Executioner was already reaching out with his left hand to grab the barrel, directing the stream of bullets toward Lupin's legs. At the same time his right hand pulled the knife from his pocket and flipped open the blade. He swung forward, stabbing the guy with the machine gun in the throat, rotating the blade as he tore it loose.

Bolan's right shoulder barreled into Lupin's chest, knocking him backward. The INTERPOL man dropped the Beretta as he grabbed his wounded legs. Bolan crouched down and threw the knife overhand at the man holding Grimaldi on the right. The blade sank into the assailant's right eye socket and he reeled back, hands flailing.

Grimaldi used this opportunity to elbow his other captor as he brought a right cross around and smashed Paco's face. The thin tour guide swung his knife at Grimaldi, striking his shoulder. Grimaldi gripped the handle of the SIG Sauer, which was still tucked into the front of Paco's pants. An explosive noise burst forth and a dark stain welled up at the man's crotch. Grimaldi pushed him back, SIG Sauer now in hand, and shot the assailant he'd elbowed, then the other one, who still had Bolan's knife projecting from his face.

The Executioner picked up his Beretta and shot Paco in the chest and then the third man in the head. He trained his pistol on Lupin, who was writhing in the sand, the blood pumping from the leg wounds. Bolan held the Beretta to Lupin's face and patted the INTERPOL man down. He found Lupin's Walther and cell phone, the ignition key to the plane and his own satellite phone. Bolan pocketed everything. Grimaldi was busy kicking weapons away from each of their dead former assailants as he checked each one for signs of life.

"These four are all dead," Grimaldi said.

Both of Lupin's legs were showing signs of arterial bleeding. Bolan stripped off the INTERPOL man's belt and tied off the right leg, and then told Grimaldi to take off Paco's belt.

"You oughta let him bleed to death," Grimaldi said as he jerked Paco's belt free of his body.

"How bad is it?" Lupin asked, clenching his teeth after he spoke.

Grimaldi tossed the belt to Bolan.

"If we don't get you to a hospital soon, you'll bleed to death," Bolan said, looping the belt above the wounds and cinching it tight.

Lupin nodded. "It is what I deserve, as the Duke says."

"Who are you working for?" Bolan asked. "Tell us and we'll get you to the hospital."

Lupin looked at him and managed a small laugh. "We both know it is too late, do we not, *mon ami*?"

Bolan turned to Grimaldi. "Give me a hand getting him to the boat."

Grimaldi nodded and grabbed Lupin's left arm. As they hoisted him, the tension on the belts slackened and the blood began to flow once again. By the time they got to the boat, Lupin was groaning in agony.

"Please, please, set me down," he said. "Only for a moment."

Bolan and Grimaldi lowered him into the boat, then Bolan retightened the tourniquets. Lupin's breathing was becoming shallow, and his eyelids drooped. It was hard to tell in the paleness of the moonlight, but Bolan figured the man had only a few minutes more.

"Who was paying you to kill us?" Bolan asked.

Lupin shook his head. "It is strange now…the pain, it is almost gone. I feel tired, but there is no pain."

"Lupin, who paid you to set us up?" Bolan said. "Who were you working for?"

"The Russians," Lupin said. "They… I feel so tired now."

Bolan tapped the man's cheek lightly. "Come on, François, tell me. The Russians…what are they after? What have they got planned?"

A dreamy look formed on Lupin's face. "I guess you will find out when you get to New York."

The serene expression slackened and Lupin's eyes glazed over.

Bolan checked the man's neck for a carotid pulse.

"He dead?" Grimaldi asked.

Bolan nodded.

"Good."

They lifted the INTERPOL man's body out of the boat and carried him back to the other bodies. Grimaldi put on his night vision goggles and scanned the area.

"Looks like we're alone," he said. "For now."

"Let's keep it that way," the Executioner replied. "We've got an appointment in New York."

15

Russian Embassy
New York City

STIEGLITZ SAT ALONE by the telecommunications set-up, but he did not dare use the wide-screen computer-phone hookup. Instead, he took out his satellite phone and dialed the number. He wasn't looking forward to yet another conversation with the voice on the other end, even if he was now an ocean away. The vise began squeezing his gut once again as he waited and listened to the ringing. Finally, it was answered.

"Everything is set?" the voice asked.

"Yes, sir. I am making the final preparations for my presentation."

Stieglitz was going to address the World Diamond Council conference in three hours. His speech would precede the auction.

"Has everything arrived safely?" the voice asked.

"Yes, sir." While Grodovich, Mikhal and Martinez were being treated to a breakfast fit for a king, Rovalev was in another part of the building being instructed on how to properly set the timer and use the low-frequency radio transmitter that would detonate the bombs. It had been fitted inside a slightly oversized briefcase. The two larger suitcases, one for each end of the long diamond assessment tables, had been delivered and packed with the cesium-137, the Semtex and the bottles of water, which would magnify the explosive force and spread the radioactivity farther.

Stieglitz swallowed with some difficulty. It was imperative that he be out of the building when the bombs detonated. He planned on leaving right after his speech. The auction was on the eighth floor and Rovalev would be on the seventh setting the timer. He could make his own way down and leave once the timer was set. The eighth floor auction area was particularly well suited to contain the blast because the walls were located in the center of the building and, hence, windowless. But the effects of the radiation would linger in the blast site for the next thirty years, at the very least.

Thirty years wasn't forever, but it was close enough.

The television images showing smoke billowing from a building in the Manhattan skyline would be enough to send the city into total chaos. And the most beautiful part was that the act would be attributed to the Chechens. Another Muslim country bent on striking the United States.

"And the breadcrumbs?" the voice asked.

"They were left to attract the mice," Stieglitz answered.

Breadcrumbs…code for the theft of the medical cesium from the Brighton Beach hospital the night before. The real supply of cesium-137 had been delivered to the embassy in diplomatic pouches three days before.

"Very well," the voice said. "I expect to hear from you when your speech has been completed."

He glanced at his watch: 8:09 a.m. In little more than six hours it would be over. Or rather just beginning. When the sun rose over the Kremlin tomorrow, it would be shining on a new Russia, one out from under the yoke of American economic oppression.

The West will soon learn, he thought, that diamonds aren't forever.

"AH, NEW YORK, NEW YORK," Grimaldi said as he started a slow descent. "The city that never sleeps. You know, I've got some Macy's coupons that are about to expire."

Bolan felt a wave of satisfaction as the Manhattan skyline became visible. Knowing they were back on American soil and had almost caught up to their quarry renewed his energy. It had taken them the better part of thirty-six hours to manage a discreet exit from Venezuela and transportation back to the United States. This was their final leapfrog.

Bolan took out his sat phone and made a quick call back to Stony Man Farm.

Brognola answered even before the first ring had been completed.

"Where are you guys?"

"Just outside the Big Apple," Bolan said. "We should be landing at LaGuardia in a few minutes. You find out anything more on Grodovich?"

"Yeah, a couple of interesting items. First, he's scheduled to unveil some big diamond he's been bragging about at the auction today. It's set for fourteen-hundred hours."

Bolan glanced at his watch: 1139. That gave them about two and a half hours to get into downtown Manhattan, find Grodovich and figure out what was happening.

"And that ain't all," Brognola continued. "It seems your buddy François never pushed through any pickup order at INTERPOL, which explains how Grodovich got out of Belgium so easily. We managed to go through *appropriate channels* to get that done." He chuckled.

"Just so we can grab him and turn him over to the NYPD," Bolan said. "But I still need to figure out what this whole thing is about. It's gone from one mystery to another all the way down the line."

"Well, don't expect a lot of assistance from the boys in blue," Brognola said. "They've got their hands full. The whole department's on alert."

"What's up?"

Brognola sighed. "First, there was a shooting in Brighton Beach. A dead Chechen gangster. And if that wasn't enough, a hospital discovered the theft of some cesium-137 from its radiological stockpile and a security guard had been killed. The antiterrorism squad went into high gear, anticipating the possibility that the cesium might be used in a radiological dispersion device."

"A dirty bomb?" Bolan said. "Any idea who was behind the theft?"

"The NYPD's keeping this one close to their vest, which is understandable. Aaron's working on hacking into some sensitive databases to try and get more info."

"As soon as we grab Grodovich, we'll pitch in and give them a hand."

"I was hoping you'd say that," Brognola said. "I don't need to tell you what havoc a dirty bomb going off in New York would cause."

Bolan did a quick mental assessment. Brighton Beach was famous for its large ethnic population, especially Russians. "Any possibility these two cases are related? Russians seem to be popping up at every turn."

Brognola grunted. "Don't know. Relations are strained right now, but I don't think the Russians would risk setting off World War Three by detonating a dirty bomb. They have to know we'd retaliate."

"Let's hope it doesn't come to that," Bolan said. "Hopefully, we'll find out soon enough."

The Mansfield Building
Avenue of the Americas
New York, New York

GRODOVICH WATCHED AS Stieglitz and Rovalev conferred on the other side of the hospitality suite. The two of them had been as thick as country felines curled up in a winter storm. Stieglitz was due to give his speech in less than forty minutes. At the embassy, Rovalev had been giving explicit instructions to four Russian lackeys from the embassy, who had carried up the two large, black plastic suitcases holding the diamonds. They had appeared much heavier than Grodovich would have imagined. Now the men and the suitcases were nowhere to be seen. He wondered if the large conflict diamond was in one. Rovalev carried a smaller case, the size of a briefcase only a bit thicker. Perhaps the conflict diamond was in that one. Grodovich sighed. It was almost time. He had been told how to describe the diamond and what price range he was to express to the auctioneer. In another hour or so, it would all be finished.

Martinez sauntered over with two glasses of red wine and handed one to Grodovich.

"Amigo, to your health," he said, his thick mustache curling above his white teeth in a devious smile. "And to our good fortune."

Grodovich nodded and sipped from the glass. Something didn't seem quite right. They were all here, at the diamond auction, and with the Venezuelan partnership in effect, the absence of any Kimberley Process documentation would not be a problem. The diamond, even in its uncut state, would no doubt draw an incredible price. And everyone would be happy.

Both Stieglitz and Rovalev seemed nervous, however. As if something more were at stake. Was there a wolf lurking in the field?

"Qué pasa?" Martinez asked. "Are you not happy? We are here, and the auction is due to begin in an hour and a half or so." He laughed and drained his glass. "I want another. *Y tu?"*

Grodovich held up his almost-full glass and shook his head. As soon as Martinez had gone, Grodovich turned to Mikhal, who was standing behind him like a silent bear.

The massive head looked downward.

Grodovich made a fractional gesture toward Stieglitz and Rovalev, who were still leaning next to each other and talking, their heads as close as a pair of lovers.

"We need to be especially watchful of those two," Grodovich said. "I am not sure what they're planning for us."

The giant nodded and looked toward them. Just then Stieglitz glanced over and locked eyes with Grodovich. Stieglitz held up his hand and motioned him over. He and Mikhal started to walk, but Stieglitz held up his palm, pointed to the giant and shook his head.

"He does not want me there?" Mikhal asked, his voice a low rumble, like approaching thunder.

"It is all right," Grodovich said. "I will only be a moment."

When Grodovich got there he saw that Stieglitz was sweating profusely. The underarms of his suit jacket displayed sodden half-moon spots.

"Are you all right?" Grodovich asked.

Stieglitz gave a quick nod. "Yes, yes, of course. The giant attracts too much attention." He looked around and then reached into the inside breast pocket of his suit, withdrawing the packet that had been prepared for the conflict diamond. He moved close to Grodovich and whispered, "I will give this to you after I complete my speech. Do not display it until the appropriate time, as instructed. Do you understand?"

"Yes." The man's body odor was pungent, overpowering, with a hint of perhaps something more.

"I must go to the toilet," Stieglitz said, shuffling off, holding his stomach with one hand.

Grodovich stepped back and watched him go.

"Performance anxiety," Rovalev said, a smile stretching across his face. "We are fortunate that it does not affect us in this manner, are we not?"

Grodovich smiled, too, but silently wondered if something else was upsetting Stieglitz. Even if that were the case, he had little choice but to let the last act of this drama play out.

BOLAN SAT IN the backseat of the taxi as the driver wound his way through the Manhattan gridlock. He glanced at his watch: 1343. The auction, and Grodovich's big unveiling of the conflict diamond, was scheduled to begin in about fifteen minutes. He doubted they'd make it before the event began, which might make grabbing the man problematic.

The vehicle in front of them moved perhaps six feet and then stopped again.

"Hey, buddy," Grimaldi said. "Will we get there before Christmas, or what?"

The taxi driver glanced over his shoulder. "What can I do, sir? The traffic is very heavy."

"If I was driving this hunk-a-junk I'd get us there in half the time," Grimaldi muttered to Bolan. He shook his head. "And speaking of time, cesium-137," the Stony Man pilot said quietly, "what's the half life of that stuff? A couple hundred years?"

"It depends," Bolan said. "I think it's more like thirty."

"Thirty years' worth of rads," Grimaldi said.

Something clicked in Bolan's mind. "Rad... Radiation?"

"Yeah," Grimaldi said. "Rads, you know, short for roentgens. Units of radiation. Kind of an old-fashioned term now, but..." He shrugged. "So what?"

Bolan didn't answer. He was recalling Burns's dying words: "Grodovich... Hot rocks... Rad—" Had he been trying to say radiation? At the time Bolan had assumed "hot rocks" meant "stolen." Now, he wasn't so sure.

Arkadi Kropotkan, Burns's significant other, had worked in the Bureau of Economic Affairs in the Kremlin, and Burns had said they had something significant to trade in exchange for a free pass back to the States. The theft of the cesium, the Chechen-Russian gang shootouts, the conflict diamond, the Russians pulling out all the stops to get Grodovich to the World Diamond Council conference auction... Suddenly it all made sense. Perfect but horrible sense.

"They're going to detonate a dirty bomb at the conference," he said.

"Huh? How do you figure?"

Bolan explained as quickly as possible.

"I think you nailed it," Grimaldi said, a grim expression on his face. "Damn, and we're still at least a mile or two away."

And they were still stopped in the traffic gridlock. Bolan heard a buzzing sound and glanced over his shoulder. Two motorcyclists were creeping forward between the rows of cars. He quickly opened the door of the cab, blocking their progress and stepped out.

"Department of Justice," Bolan said, flashing his identification and badge. "We need to commandeer your motorcycles."

The first biker, a yuppie type with Oakley sunglasses, peeled his lips back in defiance. "Huh? No way, man."

Bolan slipped his Beretta out of his holster and held it down by his leg. "Get off now."

Grimaldi was already moving around the rear of the taxi and pointing his SIG Sauer at the second biker. "You too, pal. It's time for you guys to do your civil duty."

"This is outrageous," the second biker said. "I want your names and badge numbers."

"Misters Beretta and SIG Sauer," Grimaldi said. "Now move."

Both of the bikers flipped down their kickstands and got off, raising their hands.

"This ain't right, man," the first biker said.

Bolan watched as Grimaldi holstered his weapon and got on the motorcycle.

"What is going on?" the taxi driver asked through the windows. "Are you robbers?"

"Federal agents," Grimaldi said.

"But what about my fare?" the taxi driver asked. "From the airport."

Bolan told both bikers to get into the cab. When they complied, he reached in his pocket and pulled out some cash. "This should get you two to the Mansfield Building. You can pick up your bikes there." He gave the money to the driver.

Grimaldi pressed the gear shift into first and popped the clutch, shooting forward. He steered between the rows of stagnant vehicles.

Bolan followed, thinking that he had fifteen minutes and counting. The clock's ticking.

The Mansfield Building
Eighth Floor

GRODOVICH STOOD WITH MIKHAL, Martinez and Rovalev outside the doors of the main conference room. The hallway was fairly wide, but except for them and a few security guards in dark blue blazers, it was empty. The conference room itself, the space in which the auction was to take place in approximately ten more minutes, was in the center of the eighth floor, with hallways on either side.

The elevator doors opened and the four men from the Embassy emerged, pushing the cart with the black and red suitcases containing the diamonds. Grodovich thought about Stieglitz and his insistence on maintaining possession of the conflict diamond until Grodovich was to enter the auction room. The man's arrogance was almost as oppressive as his body odor.

Grodovich smiled at the thought of the other man's pungency. It was no mystery why they did not want him to present the large stone. The bidding would be prematurely halted due to the offensive smell.

"We will go in soon?" Mikhal asked.

The giant had been fairly quiet since their arrival, seeming to be awestruck by the immensity of the city. Although Moscow and Antwerp had their share of tall buildings, New York was like being in a mountain range of skyscrapers.

Grodovich nodded. "Yes, soon."

Rovalev smiled. "The big bear is uneasy in these urban surroundings, eh?"

Mikhal stiffened and glared down at Rovalev. Although he and Grodovich had forged a tenuous friendship over the chess matches, he knew Mikhal did not like him very much. Perhaps the giant's sensory impressions were more prescient than Grodovich had thought.

Rovalev still carried the oversized black briefcase and had balked when Grodovich asked what was in it.

"Just some papers and certificates," Rovalev had said.

The quickness of his reply and the uneven timbre of his voice made Grodovich think the man was lying, but why? What was really in that briefcase?

AFTER SEVERAL CLOSE calls, Bolan and Grimaldi finally made their way to the Mansfield Building, going the last two blocks on the sidewalk, dodging pedestrians and attracting the attention of NYPD officers walking the downtown beat. As Bolan screeched to a halt in front of the building, two uniformed officers ran toward him, their hands on their guns.

Bolan quickly took out his Department of Justice ID and held it up, his other hand also high and away from his side. Grimaldi pulled up and did the same.

When the officers were in earshot, Bolan said, "Matt Cooper, DOJ."

The first officer slowed a bit and reached for the ID, keeping his right hand on his weapon.

"What the hell's going on?" he asked, looking at the identification.

"Get hold of your supervisor," Bolan said. "And the Anti-Terrorism Task Force. We've got reason to believe there's a dirty bomb set to go off at the diamond conference in this building."

The young officer's eyes widened. His partner, a female officer, was right beside him now.

"A dirty bomb?" the first officer said.

"Look, we don't have time to play twenty questions," Bolan said. Pedestrians were gathering now and the last thing Bolan wanted was panic. He lowered his voice. "Did you get briefed on the theft of some radioactive material being stolen yesterday?"

The officer blinked. "Yeah, at roll call."

"Well, it's here," Grimaldi said, jerking his thumb toward the building. "And we got to find it. Fast."

The officer cocked his head and grabbed his radio. "I'll call the special detail assigned to the conference."

"Tell them to get a hazmat team over here with containment equipment," Bolan said. "We'll be up on whatever floor the World Diamond Council conference is on."

With that, he and Grimaldi turned and pushed through the revolving doors.

GRODOVICH WAITED OFF to the side as people continued to filter into the large conference room. Martinez had already gone inside to get a good seat. The auction was set to begin in a scant few minutes and Stieglitz had not yet given him the large stone. From the smattering of applause after the Kremlin man's speech, Grodovich had the distinct impression that the audience was less than enthusiastic. He glanced inside to see where Stieglitz and Rovalev were. Stieglitz was talking to the Black Wolf and pointing in an animated fashion. The four men from the embassy were loading one of the suitcases onto the long row of tables where the diamond merchants sat. But there should be two cases. Where was the other one? It made little sense to keep the cases separated. In such a large room, with so many people, how could you keep track of them?

Stieglitz shot a glance toward the doors and locked eyes on Grodovich. He said something and Rovalev turned and looked, as well.

What were those two planning?

Grodovich didn't like it. Something told him he should

grab Mikhal and leave immediately, but he knew that was not a viable option. Everything he had, his money and his freedom, was still tied up in Russia, and going through with this diamond negotiation was the only path he could take.

Stieglitz and Rovalev walked out of the room. Two ushers held the doors and then closed them as they exited.

"I should be going inside," Grodovich said. "Are you going to give it to me now?"

Stieglitz pursed his lips as he reached into his pocket and withdrew the wrapped packet.

"You are clear on your instructions?" His voice was full of wariness.

"Of course," Grodovich said. He held out his hand and Stieglitz stared down at it, then firmly pressed the packet into Grodovich's palm. It was sodden with sweat.

Grodovich wrinkled his forehead. "What is this? You have perspired so much the specifications are illegible. The ink is all smeared."

"Never mind that," Stieglitz said. "Get in there. Do as I have instructed you. Now!" He gripped his stomach suddenly, then said, "I must go to the toilet."

He broke away and trotted down the hallway toward the restrooms. Rovalev, who was still holding the briefcase in his left hand, gripped the doorknob with his right and motioned with his head for Grodovich to enter the conference room.

Grodovich didn't like it. There was something they weren't telling him. He stood his ground and shook his head.

"Perhaps you have some alternate copies of the stone's specifications in your briefcase," he said, nodding at Rovalev. "Why don't you check and see?"

Rovalev was sweating, too, although not as copiously as Stieglitz. Something was definitely going on.

"Believe me, there is nothing of the sort in my case," Rovalev said, his tone gruff. He nodded at the door again. "Now, go inside and do as you were told."

Grodovich shook his head. "Not until you show me what is inside that briefcase. Open it."

Rovalev laughed, but it sounded forced. "Now is not the time for silly games." He reached out and grabbed Grodovich by the arm, pulling him toward the room.

"Release him," Mikhal said.

Rovalev frowned but removed his hand.

"Tell me what you and Stieglitz were whispering about," Grodovich said. "Is there some problem or concern with this?" He held up the packet containing the diamond.

Rovalev blew out a quick breath in obvious frustration. "Just go inside and do your fucking presentation."

"Not until you open your briefcase," Grodovich said.

"You are being stupid," Rovalev said. "Childish."

"Perhaps," Grodovich replied. "Mikhal, get me his briefcase."

The giant lumbered forward and Rovalev moved away from the doors. Mikhal pivoted with surprising quickness and reached out, grabbing Rovalev's left arm, the one holding the briefcase.

Rovalev's lips peeled back, exposing a row of glistening white teeth. Grodovich knew that Mikhal's grip was extremely powerful.

Rovalev reached inside his jacket and when his right hand emerged it was holding a pistol. He pointed it directly at Mikhal's massive chest and the pistol spat twice, the flame leaping from the barrel, the shell casings spitting outward, the acrid smell of gunpowder filling the hallway.

Grodovich looked on in horror.

Mikhal stumbled slightly, gripping his chest. Rovalev jerked his arm free, stepped out of the giant's reach, pointed the pistol at Grodovich and fired.

The round was like a red-hot iron driving into his gut. The pain came seconds later, along with a fuzziness that seemed to draw all of his focus to his own body, his hands. Red blood was soaking through the front of his shirt and his stomach looked distended. More blood spread through the fabric, and he suddenly realized he was on his knees. Rovalev was nowhere to be seen. Mikhal was struggling to his feet, the front of his blue shirt red with blood, as well. He glanced down at Grodovich with a look of concern.

Grodovich waved dismissively. "I am all right," he managed to say. "Get him. Kill him."

As the giant lumbered off down the hallway, Grodovich put his hand on the floor to steady himself. The world seemed to be tilting. He felt a strange weakness washing over him like an ocean wave, and he rolled down onto the carpet. He lay on his back, staring up at the fluorescent lights.

Funny, he thought as the pain began to emanate in a widening pattern from his center. I didn't notice those lights before…

He felt groggy and knew he was most probably going into shock.

Am I dying? he wondered.

Assuming he most likely was, he couldn't help but feel, at the same time, a small sense of satisfaction at having interfered with their master plan, whatever it was. He also felt hopeful. If Mikhal could catch that bastard, Rovalev, perhaps his assassin would be killed, as well.

FOUR SECURITY GUARDS and one of the uniformed NYPD officers escorted Bolan and Grimaldi up to the eighth floor to the World Diamond Council conference. The police officer's radio crackled with traffic. The elevator doors slid open and Bolan saw a bald man rushing toward the opening. The guy was covered with sweat and had a look of desperation spread across his face.

"Let me on this elevator," he said in heavily accented English. The man's body odor was overpowering.

"Gah-vah-reet-yet pah-roos-skee?" Bolan asked. Do you speak Russian?

"Da," the man replied, then said, "What, who… Get out of my way."

Bolan stepped out of the elevator and grabbed him. "I don't think so. We need to talk."

"Looks like a man down over there," Grimaldi said.

Bolan glanced down the hallway and saw the supine figure. He pushed the sweaty man toward the security guards and said, "Hold him."

The guards complied and the police officer immediately began patting him down.

"No, no," the man said. "I cannot stay here. It is very dangerous."

Bolan and Grimaldi exchanged glances with the cop, who immediately took out his handcuffs.

"In that case, buddy," the officer said, snapping on the bracelets, "you're gonna show us exactly where the danger is."

The man continued to yell in a mixture of Russian and English. Bolan ran over to the figure in the hallway and checked him. It was Grodovich. His breaths were coming in shallow, small gasps. The tear of a bullet hole was in the center of a growing red stain on the front of his shirt.

Bolan leaned close.

"Grodovich, where's the bomb?"

Grodovich's eyes widened and he shook his head. He

reached up and pressed a wet bundle of papers into Bolan's hand. The Executioner looked at it. Something hard, about the size of a small apple, was inside. He handed it to Grimaldi.

"Jack, check this." Turning back to Grodovich he said again, "The bomb—where is it?"

Grodovich's eyes had a glazed look now. He pointed down the hallway. Bolan saw numerous shell casings on the carpet and a definite blood trail leading toward the exit sign.

"See if you can get a location on the device," Bolan told Grimaldi.

The Executioner pulled out his Beretta and ran toward the stairs, following the trail of crimson.

He pushed open the door and chanced a quick peek.

No one on the landing. Blood droplets littered the descending staircase. Bolan flattened against the far wall, pistol extended, and began to work his way down. He moved with cautious but rapid motion, knowing that the clock was ticking.

A huge bloody footprint was smudged at the door leading to the seventh floor. Suddenly he heard the popping of several shots. He pulled open the door and glanced down the hallway.

A huge man took three lumbering steps, bounced off the wall to his right and then flopped onto the floor. Beyond him a man with jet-black hair and a short beard held a Tokarev pistol, a 9 mm from the looks of it, in his right hand and a briefcase in his left. Wisps of smoke hung in the air.

Bolan took aim and fired just as the dark, bearded man fired back. The bullet ripped the wall by the Executioner's head. He couldn't tell if his round had struck the assailant, but a flicker of recognition flashed in Bolan's mind.

The bearded man's face…on the Moscow street…the guy who'd shot Framer.

The gunman pulled open a door and ducked into a room on his left. Bolan advanced down the hallway, his Beretta held at combat ready. As he passed the prone giant he saw the huge back rising and falling in laborious fashion. It must have been his blood trail, but was he friend or foe? Or maybe both? Bolan figured the giant was Grodovich's associate from Krasnoyarsk prison. The bearded man had probably shot Grodovich and this guy.

The bomb intruded into his thoughts. It was most likely on the floor above from the way the bald Russian was trying to vacate the area. And the briefcase the bearded man carried…the detonator?

Pausing at the room, Bolan tried the doorknob.

Locked.

The door itself was solid wood and he noted it opened outward. That meant trying to kick it in would be futile. His only chance was to destroy the locking mechanism. He adjusted the selection lever to full auto and sprayed the area next to the doorknob, figuring that the solid wood would stop any rounds from the Tokarev coming from inside the room. The same couldn't be said for the walls. The wood between the knob and the jamb disintegrated, and the Beretta's slide locked back. As Bolan dropped the magazine to reload, the door burst open, knocking the Executioner back.

The bearded man pressed his Tokarev against Bolan's chest. It fired three times, each bullet feeling like a kick from a mule as they jammed against Bolan's Kevlar vest. He smashed the still empty Beretta against the side of the bearded man's face several times. Blood ran down from his temple.

They rolled over and Bolan released his grip on his Beretta and grabbed for the Tokarev. As his hand gripped it he realized its slide was locked back, as well.

Two empty guns.

The bearded man kneed Bolan in the groin. The pain and nausea danced upward, but the Executioner fought it off and smacked his fist into the side of the bearded man's head. They rolled over again, each struggling for a dominant position.

Bolan managed to use his legs to kick the man off of him. The man rolled to his feet with the grace of a gymnast. Bolan stood, too, bringing his arms up to block a high roundhouse kick from his opponent. Bolan shot out a kick of his own, but the bearded man moved out of range. He smiled as he advanced, an expression of utter confidence on his face.

Bolan's left side ached, each breath accompanied by a numbing pain. He switched to a southpaw stance, keeping the injury farther away. The bearded man feinted with a front kick, then swiveled his body, snapping a roundhouse that smashed into Bolan's left arm and chest. His injured ribs were on fire.

The Executioner shot a right jab at the bearded man, clipping his cheek.

The man swung a left hook over the jab and caught Bolan on the temple. The soldier's legs wavered for a millisecond, then he delivered a one-two punch to the other man's body. The man swung with an uppercut, but Bolan slipped it. As the punch whizzed by, he delivered a solid right hook to the bearded face.

His opponent sagged slightly, spitting blood, but then came right back, grabbing Bolan and smashing a knee into the Executioner's side. His injured side. Bolan gritted his teeth and gripped his opponent's jacket. *Harai Goshi*, the sweeping hip throw, flashed through Bolan's mind, and he pivoted and executed the judo move.

The man flipped over Bolan's back, landing on the floor.

Bolan tried to kick him in the head, but he rolled away, countering with a punch aimed at Bolan's groin.

The Executioner twisted his leg to absorb the impact. It still felt like getting hit on the thigh with a ball-peen hammer. He sent another kick at his opponent and this time caught the bearded man in the chest as he was rising, sending him backward. He rolled over and away, coming up about four feet back with Bolan's discarded Beretta and the full magazine.

A glint of triumph shone on the bearded man's face as he hit the ejection button, dropping the spent magazine, and inserted the full one. He pulled once on the end of the slide, sending it forward and chambering a fresh round.

"This time I aim for your fucking head," the man said, spit shooting from his torn lips as his arm straightened with the Beretta.

Before Bolan could react a huge hand grabbed the bearded man's right foot and jerked him off his feet. He fell face-first to the floor as a mountain moved behind him and huge fists rained down on the bearded man's back and head. But he rolled over, pointed the Beretta at the giant and fired. The big man continued to throw punch after punch, the front of his shirt a field of torn, bloody holes. His movements slowed and the bearded man kicked away from him, twisting to point the pistol in Bolan's direction.

As the bearded man turned the Executioner threw his Espada knife, the blade sinking into his throat. He lurched to the side, hitting the wall. Bolan lunged forward and ripped the Beretta from the other man's hand.

The Executioner pointed the pistol at the top of the

bearded man's head and pulled the trigger. His assailant collapsed to the floor. As rapidly as he could, Bolan shuffled down the hall to the room and pulled open the door. The briefcase sat open on a desk. Bolan moved over to it and saw that it was some kind of radio transmitter. The dials had been set to a certain frequency and a panel of lights flickered, one of them displaying the red numerals of a descending countdown.

0009…0008…0007…

Bolan scanned the transmitter for a kill switch.

0006…0005…

Seeing none he raised the Beretta, pointed it toward the mechanism and pulled the trigger several times. Sparks flew as the jacketed rounds drove through the plastic and metal, and the screen depicting the red numerals suddenly went black.

Bolan waited about ten seconds more…

No big bang from upstairs.

He let out the breath he'd been holding.

Epilogue

Stony Man Farm

BOLAN SLOWLY LOWERED himself into a chair on the near side of the conference table in the War Room, across from Brognola. Grimaldi sat beside him. A network of creases and wrinkles spread over Brognola's face as he looked across the table.

"How are your ribs?" he asked.

"Sore," Bolan said. "But, thanks to Kevlar, without any accompanying holes."

Brognola nodded. "Well, I thought I owed you guys an update."

"Actually, you owe us a helluva lot more than that," Grimaldi said. "But who's keeping track?"

Brognola laughed. "Well, as you probably figured out, the Russians are denying the whole thing."

"What?" Grimaldi said. "How can they do that? Those were Russians we caught trying to set off that dirty bomb."

"True," Brognola said, "but here's the kicker. The Kremlin is saying it just broke up a ring of Chechen terrorists who claimed responsibility for the bombing at the WDC conference. They've sent a copy of the video to our State Department. The foiled attack was supposedly in retaliation against Grodovich and the Russian government for the murders of his ex-partner, Yuri Kadyrov, and the Robies. Apparently they were all Chechen nationals, with the exception of Yuri, who was half Russian."

"And the guy with the transmitter?" Bolan asked. "You find out anything about him?"

"Just another Russian mercenary working for the highest bidder," Brognola said. "Again, according to the Russians."

"What a bunch of horseshit," Grimaldi said. "And believe me, I know horseshit when I smell it."

Brognola laughed. "I'll bet you do."

"Seems kind of farfetched that the Chechens would have the reach," Bolan said.

"Yeah," Grimaldi added. "And what about that smelly son of a bitch?"

"Vassili Greggor Stieglitz," Brognola said. "A cabinet member of the Bureau of Economic Affairs in the Kremlin."

"We're going to prosecute him, right?" Grimaldi said.

Brognola looked down at the table and shook his head fractionally. "He was released two hours after you guys grabbed him."

"What?"

"The Russians asked for him to be returned under the provision of diplomatic immunity," Brognola said. "The President had no choice."

"More horseshit," Grimaldi said.

"You know how things work, Jack," Bolan said. "Don't let it get to you."

"Aww, I knew I should've clipped that little SOB when I was holding him for the coppers." Grimaldi shook his head.

"Even the worst rain cloud can have a silver lining," Brognola said. He leaned forward and pressed a button on the remote and the large screen rolled downward. Brognola pressed another button and the overhead projector clicked on. "I was saving the best for last. I got this from a source inside the Agency. He knows a guy, who bribed a guy, who has a source at Krasnoyarsk prison."

He clicked his mouse and a picture of three men appeared. All were dressed in the black prisoner garb of Detention Center Six. One of the men was bald and the other two, both powerfully built, were holding his arms with wide grins on their faces. The bald man's face held a look of sheer terror.

"Is that who I think it is?" Grimaldi asked.

Brognola nodded. "Your buddy Stieglitz."

"Looks like the Russians had him pegged as their perfect fall guy," Bolan said. "In case the best-laid plans went wrong."

"Yeah," Brognola said. "Their president made a personal call to ours saying how he had rooted out the terrorist corruption in his cabinet and so on and so forth. Stieglitz was just their patsy."

"That poor bastard." Grimaldi clucked sympathetically. "I guess he didn't get away with much after all. You know, I almost feel sorry for him."

"And then, there's this." Brognola opened his briefcase and pulled out an item wrapped in newspaper. Unpeeling it, he took out the murky stone that Grodovich had given Bolan.

"It's a synthetic," Brognola said. "Still valuable but not worth as much as a natural diamond."

"Just like I always say," Grimaldi said. "Diamonds aren't forever."

"Unlike the forever war of good against evil," Bolan said as he pushed himself up from the chair. It was time to get back to it.

* * * * *